MW00634712

When Women Danced With Trees

35 UNEXPECTED STORIES

MARINA BROWN

Gilberte
Publishing

Published by:
Gilberte Publishing
5377 Paddington Drive.
Tallahassee, FL 32309

ISBN- 978-0-9897543-5-4

Some of these stories were originally published in the St. Petersburg Times (now Tampa Bay Times), the Tallahassee Democrat, and selected anthologies.

Printed in the United States of America
First Edition September 2021

PRAISE FOR

When Women Danced With Trees

"An amazing collection! An eclectic & beautiful set of stories and tales!"

— Donna Meredith, Assoc. Editor, Southern Literary Review

"Before you leap into Marina Brown's vivid world, best secure your parachute. Like the most skilled short story masters O. Henry or Chekhov, or even a master mixologist, at the end of the rainbow you will invariably find a tart twist of lime. Or wit. Or both. With a word palette that sings with a blend of color and insight, the reader of this unique collection of Marina Brown short stories may feel like Dorothy who opens the door of her drab Kansas farmhouse to a brilliant Technicolor Oz."

— Susan Ellen Gross. Author of *The Midnight Fury* and other novels

"I'll always remember the first time I read a Marina Brown story. I had just been hired as editor and I read a story she had written about a Tallahassee church. I was transported from my home in Fort Walton Beach into that sanctuary many miles away. I could hear the singing, feel the wood pews and see the faithful gathered all through the word pictures of a talented writer and storyteller. You don't just read a story written by Marina Brown. You feel it and join her in the journey".

— William Hatfield, Executive Editor, Tallahassee Democrat

"Marina Brown's stories are an unconfined and entrancing examination of the human condition!"

— Steve Bornhoft, Executive Editor, Rowland Publishing.

"These stories are powerful gems! And gorgeous. With each story different from the next, through Marina Brown's keen eye and brilliant imagination, we meet women who find solace in trees—images that will haunt you for days. Or we are drawn into a profound story of whale bones that carry their own truth. Marina Brown's writing, as in her novels, is always vivid, stirring, and filled with imaginative twists. A book to keep and to ponder."
— Claire Matturro, author of *Wayward Girls* and other books.

"This collection is a treasure chest of stories! Marina Brown's imaginative and descriptive powers sweep across genres, inviting us to laugh, weep, and observe the nuances of the human condition through the lens of her elegant prose."
— Barbara Palmer, Art Historian

"Marina Brown's lush descriptions and imagery, her metaphors of daily life become artistry, painted with words."
— Fran Conaway, Past President, Osher Life Long Learning Institute

"Magnificent tales! With nods to the magically real that in fact bring the reality of our days into focus, Brown makes us both laugh and cry—with language that could light the night."
— Jeremy Dorsey, Crofton Books, London.

Acknowledgements

For this eclectic gathering of stories from near and far, happy to sad, and just at the fuzzy border of what is possible, I wish to thank—first of all, Life itself. I have been richly blessed with experiences that lead to imagination, that have led back to a written reality. And I am grateful.

And grateful too for my husband, Doug Kiliman, who has offered up so many hours in his gentle critiques, in the preparation of my drawings, the refining of the cover, and in the precise organization of this work for publication. He is the "lion" of Gilberte Publishing.

My heartfelt thanks as well to the wonderful readers of early drafts for their "professional eyes," readers who could catch spelling errors and wayward commas, and offer encouragement in the process: the beloved Claire Matturro, the oh-so-knowledgeable Donna Meredith, supportive Barbara Palmer, dear Sue Gross, and the literary pros, Editors Steve Bornhoft, and William Hatfield.

Thanks to you all!
Marina Brown

.

Other Books by Marina Brown

Land Without Mirrors
Walking Alone Together
Airport Sketches
Lisbeth
The Leaf Does Not Believe It Will Fall
The Orphan of Pitigliano

Dear Reader,

Although writers may categorize themselves according to where their work is published—newspaper journalist, magazine writer, poet, short story specialist, or novelist—in the end, it is the ability of the *written word* to paint a picture that has hooked us, words that are as real and vibrant as reality—no matter the genre in which we write.

We are "writers" of pictures. Moving pictures that carry us along, both the writer and the reader, and if we're lucky, drop us off someplace different from where we started. Hopefully we'll find ourselves smarter, sadder, more amused, or more joyful than when we hitched that ride with the author.

Though I mainly write novels, and for the other media too—the collection here is an outgrowth of the stories I've written ever since my teacher had me read my "suspense-filled, African tale" in second grade. A number of stories have been published elsewhere—especially the stories about exotic places. Many of them are inspired by my own life's observations—sometimes only a passing stranger's expression, a mattress store I pass on the road, my years spent sailing, or a Tallahassee lake where God only knows what goes on at night.

None of the stories is long. But long enough, I hope, that you will find the people you meet here interesting. Maybe you will marvel at their circumstances, occasionally laugh out loud at their antics, or sometimes weep along with them—always remembering that inside a book, anything—absolutely *anything* is possible.

Yours, with best wishes to enjoy every word,
Marina Brown 2021

THE STORIES

JUST DESERTS—SERVED WITH A TWIST
The Day Doug Fell Overboard 3
The All-Night Mattress Store 8
Dining Out at Lake Overstreet 11
What They Don't Tell You About the AARP 20
A Fair Exchange 27

LOST AND FOUND
Arnold and the Lady 43
Merry Christmas from George 49
Take Your Shot 53
The Joy of Peeing in Your Pants 56
Lift Every Hand 65

HOPEFUL, SWEET, AND SCARED SPITLESS
The Other Side of the Parking Lot 75
Pandemic: Month Eleven 77
The Sweetness of Red Cabbage 80
Stage Fright in the Time of COVID 83
The Physics of Nations 85

WHEN LIFE IS NOT KIND
A Love Song 91
Upon a Midnight Clear 95
The Flower Box 97
The Middle Years 104
The White Swan 108

THE STORIES, continued

MAGICALLY REAL

Deep Dive at Lake Overstreet.. 119

"To You As Well, Signore" 129

May I Have This Dance? 131

The Graceful Arts 135

When Women Danced With Trees.. 141

GETTING AWAY FROM IT ALL

Accursed Bones 151

Aegina and the Man in a Box 159

One Earth's Turn in Tanzania 163

Being Kuna... 166

The Artisans of Florence 173

Holy Ethiopia! 179

Golden Bangles, Silver Moons, Swirling Scarlet Saris..... 184

My Ghost 190

All Through the Night 195

Italy Is Where… 201

JUST DESERTS — SERVED WITH A TWIST

The Day Doug Fell Overboard

To a woman who'd been skirting the outer edges of sleep, it sounded as if someone had dropped a large piece of crystal whose exploding fragments now scattered the floor. Still in her dream, Barbara picked up and examined a large shard, and realized that any one of the evil-looking pieces could successfully pierce the sleep into which she'd so thankfully lapsed.

And then it came again. The sound this time more powerful. Barbara Roberts jerked to her elbow, eyes wide open in the dark. She heard the lapping waves softly hitting the yacht's blue hull and felt the gentle cradle of the boat's motion, but she was still not far from her dream. The dream where she was back at home. Where a cup of coffee stayed put when you sat it on a table. Where she could fix her hair or put on mascara without wind or rain intervening. Back where she could listen to a string quartet and go to the theatre, or eat something besides potluck with people other than "yachties"—strangers she didn't want to know. Barbara literally dreamed of a place where there were topics of conversation other than the broken things on boats.

A machine's gravelly din was beginning to subtly shake her bed, as if the initial "crashes" were a clearing of the motor's throat so that it could now belt out its mechanical ballad in a raucous "Louie Armstrong" imitation. Barbara sank back down on the bunk, realizing it was hot in the cabin and that the bedsheets were uniformly moist. She remembered the crystal shards again, still reverberating in her head. "I loved that vase," she thought, picturing the fancy cut-glass piece with an inscription etched at the bottom. "Let's see, that was given to me for chairing the Artist's Ball in 1998." She closed her eyes, trying to visualize her name in fancy script and almost immediately she saw the vase tip and roll onto its

3

fat belly and from there onto the floor. "Yes," she said, sitting up in the dark, aware that any thought of sleep was over. "That's what would happen if I had that vase here. Like everything else, it would break."

The dull drone abruptly stopped, and in the next second a thunderous mechanical surge that shook the entire vessel stood Barbara bolt upright, wide awake now, and angry. "What the hell time is it, anyway?" she said out loud, already knowing the sound of the mammoth generator was perversely switched on by six. No need now to check on where Doug was either. No Doug, no noise, and vice versa.

Feeling for the cabin sole with her toes, Barbara reached for a grab rail and pulled herself away from the bunk. It was stifling in the master cabin. Situated at the stern of the boat, the owners' cabin was roomy alright, but placed so that no moving air ever reached it. Doug wouldn't consider sleeping anywhere else, even with just the two of them onboard. It had been like this for the two years they'd been living on the yacht. "It wouldn't be proper for the owners to sleep on deck," he'd said. She'd often puzzled over the dichotomy between Doug's pride and his resolute cheapness. Hell, they could have the air-conditioning on. She could use gallons of water. They could even dock the boat at an upscale marina. They were anything but poor. But instead, Doug preferred that everyone suffer. No A/C; two liters of water per person per day; and a dropped anchor away from all the restaurants and fun. That was Doug's way. And the only way.

In the dark, she located her watch and pushed the tiny illumination button. Five-thirty. "Damn," she muttered. She could feel the rivulets of sweat begin to roll out from under her breasts. Barbara reached up and stripped off the soggy T-shirt she'd been wearing, and flinging it onto the bunk, had a mental flash of a piece of soft satin and lace lingerie—the kind she wore at home—flying through the dark. Something from a long, long time ago, she noted sadly.

The sound of the generator suddenly ended. Maybe Doug had completed its daily run-regimen, and with a glass of cool water, she might just get back to sleep.

Barbara inched forward in the dark cabin. She needed to step over the elevated divider between the sleeping and bathroom areas. She poked her foot forward like a probe, feeling left, then right. But with the sudden thunderous cacophony of Doug starting up the generator for the second time, Barbara's little toe caught on the outside of the head's wall and she pitched forward into the dark. Totally disoriented, she felt herself falling, grasping for anything, and she nearly did catch herself on the sink. But her hands were wet with perspiration, and she plunged instead headlong into the bathroom and into the space between the wall of the hull and the handle for pumping the toilet. As if packed for shipping, Barbara was now held perfectly and securely by the boat, battened down against any possible spontaneous movement. In that position, with the side of her head pressed tightly against the vessel's hull, and the long handle pressing into her back, she could feel the generator's power throbbing through fiberglass and her own cartilage and bone and into her brain—like a dentist working on a cavity from the inside.

Barbara tried to lift her arms for a purchase to push up, but her left shoulder was forced down and helpless, and the other arm could only flail uselessly in the air, or slam against the bathroom wall.

"Doug!" she yelled. "Doug! Help! Goddamn him," she pounded and cursed, so far from the genteel, polite, and sensitive woman she believed to be her core self. Barbara had always believed in a secret person inside, the one tucked deep down, the marrow of self, the one that was never really touched by current circumstances. But right now, pinned half-naked, dripping with sweat, in a pitch-black cabin, the roar of the generator blasting against her head, and Doug—Doug attending, like he always did, to his machines instead of her, well, damn, it was hard to go back to that quiet and serene place.

Barbara remained still for a moment, out of breath and pushing wet hair away from her face with her free hand. The air smelled of diesel and the bilge. She wondered how long she would be here. Would he notice she was missing? She wondered if Doug had a mental place like she had for regenerating herself. She hoped so. It would be nice to go there together. Nice to find a place where she would come first ahead of alternators and roller furling. Where she could let him see the playful girl, the funny, vivacious woman, with the sensual, poetic spirit, and believe he'd care if that spirit lived or died; or was at least worth putting off re-caulking the portholes for.

Barbara began to bang harder on the hull. Her left shoulder was really hurting now. "I wonder if I'm bleeding? What if it's broken?" she thought. "He'll kill me if I can't crank the winches. Maybe I'll have to be sent home." Her thoughts were wandering all over the place, and it was so hot. The generator's whine revved up and down like a swarm of insects, momentarily lulling her into an unnatural sleep, and then she heard a new, but familiar noise. From the main salon came the oddly staccato robotic voice she heard every morning: "Calling all stations. Calling all stations. This is the United States Coast Guard, New Orleans branch. NOAA weather channel 13876 and USCG position 35JC4 for weather located at 54.65 North and 43.94 South to latitude 23.38 West and 74.39 East." The electronic voice had a guttural accent as if the electronic weather man were from a distant mid-European country.

Barbara knew that the VHF weather would last at least twenty minutes. Doug would sit staring at the controls, doodling figures of weather over areas thousands of miles from where they were, but he just liked the idea of knowing, as if knowing would give him control over where he was. Control was almighty important to Doug, God knew.

From time to time, Barbara would wiggle and squirm and push with her one good arm in an effort to screw herself out of the impossible position. But she felt herself growing weaker. She was dying for a glass of water now. Her left arm was numb, her neck was aching, and both legs had gone to sleep. She launched into another refrain of screams, trying to rise above the high-pitched, mechanical European in the salon, and Louis Armstrong in the engine room, but eventually, her calls turned to tears and then to spasmodic sobs.

Barbara was splashing in a fountain in Italy. She was back in college during that wonderful study-abroad summer. It was a silly night of Spumanti-induced giggling and kissing that had ended in all of them sitting in a fountain under the fine stream from a lion's granite mouth, simply enjoying the cool water tracking down their faces and along their arms. She was so glad she'd gone back there—except that this water was warm.

"Doug!! Doug!! Stop!! Stop!!" she yelled, spitting the liquid out of her mouth and trying to cover her head with her one good arm. "What the hell!" she heard him say. Doug reached over and switched on the light.

"What in God's name are you doing down there!" He was angry. When things weren't the way they should be, you could be sure Doug would be angry and profane. He finished urinating, at least aiming a little more to the left. "Why didn't you turn on the light? This wouldn't have happened if you'd turned on the light," he said accusingly. "Just help me get up," she said. Doug was looking down at the toilet as Barbara again twisted to get free, demonstrating how impossible it was without help.

"You've really caused a big problem here," he said like a mechanic scolding a particularly stupid driver who never thought to change the oil. "Your back is wedged so that I can't even pull down the lever to flush the commode." He grabbed the long handle of the toilet and shoved it up and down, each time letting the downward stroke bang into Barbara's back. "See," he said, disgustedly. "Now, I'm somehow going to have to take the whole filthy bowl off." She closed her eyes. She wanted to be back in Italy.

"Better get ready to get wet," she heard him say as he went down the companion way for his tools.

And it was later in the day, after Doug fell overboard, that Barbara again began to hear the strains of Verdi.

The All-Night Mattress Store

Don't tell me I look pathetic. Just don't. Or that if I didn't get up and change positions, I'd be like a character out of an Edward Hopper, flat-liner, diner painting. No way. I am not depressed. I do not sit with my back to the plate glass window forever hunched over a cup of stale coffee, nor do I chew breath mints in the hope of charming a customer who might show up, intoxicating him or her with a little cloud of spearmint.

And so what if it's high noon and I haven't made a sale? So what if Beth and Sid are pulling down the big commissions on the Softee Tops and Spine-Aligners? Hell, did anyone ever look at Beth's big butt and Sid's scoliosis. Oh, sure, Beth got a free mattress for being "tops in sales." Yeah, and I'll bet she lays on that damned Softee 12 hours a night just picturing the rest of us sunk in our old sprung beds. Well, that's what your butt looks like when you do that.

Naw, I tell the customer what's really good for them. Which mattress is the one for a real night's sleep. If only there were a few more of them—customers—real ones, I mean. Not what I get. Not what I have to deal with. Take last night.

It was about midnight. I'd been standing, sitting, walking, fluffing since I came on at seven. Like we're hospital interns, they have us do 12-hour shifts. So, there I am, fired up on double espressos, turning mattresses just for the hell of it, laying on the Adjust-a-Backs in the corner and running them up and down in a futile effort to make myself dizzy, and for the last half hour, playing handball off the back wall.

Then in walks Herzog. Now Herzog is a nice old guy, about 70 I'm guessing by the look of his beard. He's what you call an Orthodox—a Jewish guy. Lonely. He wears a big black hat and a

8

black coat and he's got these long Shirley Temple ringlets hanging down in front of his ears. Sometimes when he can't sleep, he'll bring me in a blintz. Nice guy. But last night, old Herzog had a problem. Turns out the old boy likes chewing gum. As a kid, his ancient mother had always had him stick it behind his ear when he went to bed… kind of a "waste not" proposition, I'm guessing. So now old Herzog, who's been in a chewing gum rut for a long time, has got his damned gum wadded into his beard hair, his neck hair, and a gooey mess in his Shirley Temple. And he wants me to help him get it out. So, what am I going to do?

Well, I need a little room to maneuver, so I lay Herzog down on the 12" PlushBaby and start picking through all those little hairs. I actually had to straddle him to get at the ones down his back. Damn, looked like he'd been rolling in chewing gum. Then, for no apparent reason the vibrating MuscleToner System turns itself on. Jesus, it was hard just hanging on. Who knew a mattress could pound a guy like that?

That's when I heard the kitty. At least I thought it was a cat—maybe snuck in and got stuck in one of the cheaper innerspring models. But it got louder and soon was meowing in unison with the MuscleToner action. I looked up, and it wasn't a cat at all.

So the tattooed girl and her skinhead boyfriend, who later told me they'd been living on the streets since they got evicted last week, said they'd seen Herzog and me going at it and decided they needed a little private time too. I didn't understand what they meant, but who am I to pass judgment? I mean, could be me without a mattress next time. While I continued vibrating old Herzog's gum out of his beard, I just told them to move to the Serta behind the pillar. What the hell, I was in need of a little company.

And I was soon to get it. First came the singing. Way off key. I noticed that because I'd been teaching myself to play guitar from 3AM to 6. But when the whole band of them walked in the door they let loose. Octaves be damned.

Now I've seen street corner evangelists, but these folks had rounded up a cadre, a posse, a platoon of the homeless whose voices and stink were rising to high heaven. I jumped off Herzog, leaving him shaking on the MuscleToner, and rushed over to the new arrivals. You never know, my boss had told me, "In the middle of the night, you just never know who might want to buy a mattress."

"We're looking for the milk of human kindness," the head preacher said. "You got any here?" At first, I didn't understand. We're a mattress store. Don't carry edibles. But then he made it clear that the down-and-outers not only needed a bath, but as he called it, "a flop." Well, why not, I thought. Half these mattresses will be sent back to the warehouse without anybody ever trying them out. So I just said, "Welcome, and to try not to vomit on anything." That's when I heard old Herzog yelling.

I looked over, and the skinhead was beating Herzog with the Tempra-Pedic remote control. Now it probably had gum all over it, I reasoned, annoyed. But before I could get to the old Jew, he'd hauled off and flattened the tattooed guy with the mock-up box spring display of a Sealy Extra-Hard. Damn, I knew those things could be lethal from dropping one on my toe.

Thank goodness for the Man-of-the-Cloth, who seemed to have been integrated into the band. It wasn't long before he'd found the common denominator for all the religious and angry loners that night. I'd gone to get ice to peel the gum off Herzog's mattress, and when I came back, I think everybody was filled with the Holy Spirit. The Evangelist had little Dixie cups topped to the brim with a sacramental wine, I believe, while all the homeless, and Herzog, and the skinhead, and his tattooed girlfriend were sitting around passing the bottle from one to the other, singing at the tops of their lungs. I have to admit—it was a beautiful sound.

Only one of the homeless threw up on a mattress, but that was easily taken care of by flipping it. And the… uh… stains on another mattress, I covered with a big blue ribbon saying, "Newly-Wed Special." As for the mattress with the gum…. Well, Herzog said he'd had such a good time that night, he'd decided to buy it. I gave him a good deal though. It was my best sales night all year.

Dining Out at Lake Overstreet

Richard Larkin had had just about enough for one week—what with the company downsizing, Emma's constant teenaged belligerence, and now, the newest insult, and possibly most upsetting, having to turn in the company car. Since Phyllis had left, taking the family van with her, the company car had been a godsend. Not having it would be just one more reason to fight with his daughter over travel priorities, and to picture Phyllis in the damned van cruising around town on her way to Pilates or on her weekly circuit of shoe stores.

But at least for now, sitting on one of the solidly sedate, wooden benches facing Lake Overstreet, Richard was intent on daydreaming for an hour—letting his current turmoil subside to something resembling the resolute ripples marching across the lake's surface. Here, the quiet punctuated only by the occasional cormorant alerting the world that it had gotten a minnow, Richard felt himself reveling in the tranquility of the deserted lake, willing any other park walkers to keep on moving.

Phyllis couldn't have let a sleepy lakeside moment like this alone, he thought. By now, she'd have interrupted the shift of leaves or random a cappella of a wood thrush and launched a hundred dead-end declarations, inane, banal proclamations about dry cleaners, the neighbor's roses, why he could never make a decent cup of decaf, and usually end by accusing him of an imagined infidelity or at least a secret lust. Just thinking about her here was enough to conjure not only her image and voice, but the tight-gut feeling he'd associated with her since they first met. The doctors called it "irritable bowel". But Richard knew better—it was all Phyllis.

11

Suddenly there was movement in the reeds about ten yards away and in a place where Richard guessed there was little dry land. He sat up with a jerk, staring cautiously at the trembling rushes. He knew there were alligators in the lake, but more likely, a bird was trying to scare up lunch. "Oooh," came a little cry. An "Oooh," that all at once said, "I am little and young and human." It also contained a sound of admiration and awe.

And then it came again. "Oooh," this time with a little giggle. Richard stood up. His legs felt stiff and not just from his hour's reverie. Rather, from a self-generated inertia as he considered if he would soon have to wade into alligator-infested waters to find a sinking child. "Hey!" He stomped noisily toward the reeds. "Who's over there!?" Everything went silent for a moment. Birds froze; insects veered away; and no smart child, drowning or not, would have called back to the rough shout.

Richard walked cautiously toward the bank and stood on high ground that sloped toward the bushes. "Is anybody there needing help?" he asked more nicely, wondering if he were speaking to an alligator or himself. Then, he spotted a glimpse of pink. "Yoo-hoo," he sang now, very gently. "Everybody OK?"

"Yes, I'm fine," came the high-pitched voice of a little girl. Using both hands and her muddy feet, the child crawled out of the blind of reeds and smiled up at Richard, a tiny blonde with a very round face and precocious blue eyes. She bore not a trace of fear— of anything in the lake or out, nor of the middle-aged man in a sweat-stained broadcloth shirt and wrinkled pants.

"It's dangerous down there, don't you think?" He smiled. "Where's your mom or dad, anyway?" "Dad'll be here in a minute," the little girl said. "Dad's taking pictures of oak tree roots, I think. The more gnarled the better!" she shrugged, laughing with a sort of adult dismissal. "Dad's busy with his camera, but I couldn't wait to come to the lake to see if he would be here."

"To see if your dad has come down here?" Richard was a little confused. "No, not Dad," she said, her eyes turning toward the lake where Richard could see a faint "v" wake pattern on the water. "Not Dad, silly… the dragon."

12

For a moment, Richard wondered if he were having one of those lucid dreams, something that bordered on reality, but certainly was not. He did a quick check. Yes, it had been a cloudless morning—May had a way in North Florida of seducing you with balmy beginnings and blue skies the color of a pricey Wedgewood bowl. By three, it would go all hot and humid, cloudy, with air that seemed complicated and confused. Check again. Everything seemed as real as the sweat along his neck, yet the ambiance of the lake had shifted. The clicking beetles were busy in conversation and birds were sleepily making remarks back and forth, but without the sun to flood color into the landscape, Lake Overstreet took on a vaguely malevolent tone. Gray told its own story.

Richard looked down at the little girl, muddy legs beginning to dry chalky and white. She was like a tiny Modigliani, a flushed oval face, and faraway eyes that made him check twice for pupils. She had both hands over her eyebrows making a little ledge from under which she could survey the lake, watching the flattening wake of something that had crossed in front of them.

"What, so there's a big dragon who lives here?" smiled Richard. "Wouldn't be called Puff, now would it?" He smiled to himself, realizing that not only was his 60's joke lost on the child, but in dating himself, he suddenly felt depressed and old. It was the clouds, he guessed—or maybe just the damned van.

Suddenly the little girl gasped and pointed to a slowly moving form, a silhouette really, nearly flush with the water, but with its own contour and dorsal topography. "It's not an alligator!" she whispered. "Alligators are boring, like street cars. They just go in straight lines. Wait till you see what Russell will do if he wants."

Involuntarily, Richard took a couple of steps toward the water, as if that could get him a better view. "Be careful!" the little girl immediately hissed. She grabbed his arm and pulled him backwards. "Russell eats things... maybe even you," she giggled. The form had apparently heard something from the bank that disturbed it, and now, a massive neck began to curl upward from the water. Slowly, seeming to weigh a great deal, the coil of gray neck continued to arch higher and higher, until at last, a dripping

13

skull, furrowed and covered with indentations came into view. One glittering chartreuse eye was fixed on them both, seeming to have already been watching from below the surface. Then as delicately as the proboscis of a butterfly, the neck extended toward them. Twenty feet long if it's five, Richard gulped.

The creature was barely moving, perhaps floating its massive hulk nearer. For minutes the fully revealed back and towering head of the animal seemed suspended. But Richard was sure he saw movement in its pupils, narrowing and dilating, bringing them into focus.

The little girl seemed to be holding her breath. He'd almost forgotten her tiny hand tugging at his shirt, so absorbed in processing that he was seeing a massive, unidentified sea creature within the city limits, within miles of his house. And then she let go and began to slowly walk toward the muddy bank. Only too late did Richard realize the child was quickening her pace.

"Wait!" he snapped in a frantic whisper. "Come back!" Richard himself didn't move, guessing that he was likely the bigger target for what he now realized he was thinking of as a "dragon." He crouched down slowly and whispered again, more desperately, "Come back here. You said it eats people, didn't you?" He'd frighten her to her senses.

But the little girl turned to him with a sunny smile and said brightly, "Oh no, I just said he might eat you." She turned back to the dragon, that had now twisted its neck into what Richard sensed was an "alert" position—ready for something.

Suddenly, the little girl began to croon, "Ob la tia ur non tal. Tal kan obi spal". She said it again in a kind of low falsetto that sounded like a famous contralto Richard had once heard on the radio. She repeated the phrase, "Ob la tia ur non tal. Tal kan obi spal," again and again, walking in a little zigzag pattern toward the bank. The child fluttered her hands as she advanced, and Richard noticed the dragon's neck was moving as well.

The sheer bulk of muscle, as thick as a hundred-year-old oak, swayed gently to the dreamy rhythm of the child's lyrics, and if

Richard could believe his eyes, he'd have sworn the dragon's pupils were dilated with pleasure.

When the little girl reached the water's edge, she lifted her dress daintily with extended pinkies and carefully continued into Lake Overstreet. Richard thought he heard a ring of a bicycle bell somewhere on the park trail, and he sent out a panicky prayer that her father was coming to save her—and not the least of his selfish thoughts—to corroborate that he was indeed in the presence of a "dragon."

The child was standing stock still now, knee-deep in the water. She was no longer chanting, but almost imperceptibly, the dragon was extending its neck toward her. Like an hour hand that never seems to move, the dragon's head had come only a few feet from her. Richard's disbelief had held him paralyzed until now, but suddenly he realized that whatever was this reptilian oddity erupting out of the sludge of Lake Overstreet, he wasn't going to let it eat an innocent child.

Like a receiver for the Denver Broncos, Richard propelled himself down the bank, arms extended, eye bolted to the dragon's eye, ready to cradle the little girl's body in the crook of his elbow as he sprinted back up the bank.

But the dragon was too fast. In one razor-sharp move, the powerful neck struck forward, the scarlet mucous membrane of its mouth closing tidily over Richard's leg in an organic snap. As fast as an elastic band's recoil, Richard found himself at the apex of the dragon's reach, seeing the blur of the land around Lake Overstreet fly left and right as the creature tossed him gently in huge figure eights, high above the water.

Strangely, he felt no pain from what Richard assumed would be massive puncture wounds. But he did hear from the bank the child's contralto chirps, staccato, and with a kind of imperiousness. Now, as quickly as the dragon had heaved him into the air, it stopped, leaving Richard swinging wildly by a spittle-soaked thigh. With the rumpled tail of his shirt hanging over his face, Richard shrieked, "Make him put me down! He'll kill us both!" From far below, the little girl smiled up at Richard—or was it at the dragon—

15

and said, "Arnek. Arnek ga-doy." And Richard was lowered into the wet reeds beside the lake.

As if sobering up from a marathon drunk, he sat in the water, shaking his head back and forth. At first Richard wasn't aware of anything around him, not his sweat-saturated shirt, not the algae and leaves in his shoes, but he sensed that he was in fact alive. Then he realized the little girl was standing beside him with one chubby hand on his shoulder engaged in a conversation, or making a little speech, and that from time to time his name, "Richard,", was being used.

He could barely lift his head. He felt like he'd taken a thug's beating. But twisting to see who she was talking to, he realized the surreal circumstance hadn't changed, except that now the dragon was lying on dry land, its 40-foot tail randomly wagging back and forth and its front paws extended like a dog's. As the thing scratched behind its earhole with a rear talon, Richard could have sworn the dragon was listening to the orations of the little girl. Though its snout was impassive, it had an expressive forehead that seemed to respond with some kind of feeling, even, Richard thought, as he watched its eyes widen, or furrows form on the scaly brow— emotion.

After a few moments, the little girl turned to him. "Mr. Richard, I have explained things to Russell. I had told you to be careful, and you didn't listen, but now that he understands that you thought I might be hurt, he has decided that not only will you not be eaten, but that it will be somebody else—of YOUR choosing—who will be his next meal." She crossed her arms, a prim, thin-lipped smile across her lips, little invisible eyebrows lifted like an executive who's just closed a really good deal.

"What!" Richard said, slipping in the mud as he rose to his hands and knees. "I don't believe any of this is happening, you know. And while I may, in fact, be looking at a species that has never, ever been seen in North Florida, and while I may somehow have escaped death very recently at its claws, believe you me, I do NOT believe that you and this "dragon" are chatting–or that I get to choose his dinner entrée!" Richard looked wide-eyed from right to left. "No sir, no way, no want a part of this!" Richard scrambled to his feet, dripping water from his cuffs, and smelling exactly like the rotting vegetation he'd been sitting in. Until the dragon nipped him on the calf. "Ouch!" Richard grabbed his leg, and stumbling to one knee, he turned angrily to the dragon, then to the little girl.

"You are very lucky he's letting you choose, Richard," the girl said. "Everything has a consequence, you see." She smiled in an arch, almost schoolmarmish way. "If someone does something bad to you, you get to do a mean thing back to them. If someone does a good thing to you, you get to repay them with a good thing." Her voice was singsong, like a mantra everyone should have known. "You tried to save my life, now you get a good thing. If someone has done something bad to you, you can help them get the bad thing they deserve. It's very simple." She looked carefully at Richard. "Hasn't someone done a bad thing to you?" Her face was flat, without real inquisitiveness, but somehow her question felt more than just rhetorical.

Richard stood dripping, still a bit dazed, yet following the logic she suggested. It was almost Biblical, he thought. So that's how things work, this god-awful creature from who-the-hell knows what era, Pleistocene? Crustaceous? and this little savant are perhaps explaining to me, at this moment, in this place, one of the central mysteries of the universe. So the "golden rule," "what goes around comes around," "quid pro quo," it's all true. Richard suddenly felt a wonderful peace. Yes, for all the wrongs, the hurts, and humiliations one encounters in life, there is a goddamned justice, even if meted out by a dragon. Well, hell, he could think of some justice that needed meting right now!

"Well," he said hesitantly, "I do know someone who deserves something... uh... bad. It's somebody who did something bad to me," he said, looking down, a little overwhelmed with the power his being wronged now seemed to carry.

"Alright," said the little girl. "I'll need to translate for him, but if you want the bad thing to happen, if you want Russell to have his dinner, then you must give him something that belongs to that person, so he'll be sure to not make any mistakes."

17

Richard wondered if what he was doing was illegal. Was he setting up a contract killing—with a child as intermediary, or was he more at one with the universe than he had ever known? He reached into his pocket. Amid the soggy cleaner's ticket and a folded $10 bill, he felt for his keys. Yes, they were still there.

He pulled out the ring. Not many there, not like a janitor or anything. There was his old house key. There was his shiny new apartment key. There was one for the rental car he was driving until he could scrape up enough for some jalopy, which would take a while since Phyllis had cleaned out their bank account too. And there was the van key—the key to the vehicle that Phyllis now parked in front of the upscale townhouse where her new boyfriend lived. Richard took it off the ring, and without a moment's hesitation, handed it to the little girl. Without missing a beat, she laid it down in front of the quietly breathing dragon, who, as it roused and sniffed the key, emitted little puffs of vapor like a toy train at Christmastime.

Richard wondered what to do next. Did he need to set an appointment for Phyllis to come to the lake? Give the dragon her address? Suddenly, the animal reared up, its massive half-submerged tail lifting out of the water and with a whiplash movement, flung gallons of water onto everyone. The little girl calmly wiped water from her forehead. But something had aroused the dragon from its torpor. It rose again, this time towering over the pines surrounding the lake, and began to sway back and forth lifting one foot, then the other like the frustrated lions in the zoo. The steamy clouds now coming from its nostrils seemed heated as they hit the outside air. And—he was growling.

The little girl walked forward again and looking up, seemed intent on the reptile's low groans, a kind of menacingly punctuated hum. She looked at the beast and she looked down at the ground where the van key was still lying. Eventually, she picked it up, stared at it a moment, then brought it over to Richard.

"What's the matter?" he asked, realizing an embarrassingly great sense of disappointment creeping over him. "This other person can't be dinner, Richard," she said, holding the key up to him. "But why not?" he said with a growing sense of outrage. After all, he'd done his damned good deed and Phyllis had given him crap. "Because this key is already in use, Richard."

The little girl's look was like a boss's when he's just fired a pesky employee and is tired of making nice. It was all over and Richard could see that. But what did she mean, "It's in use"?

From behind him, Richard suddenly heard what sounded like a backhoe at work. He spun around to see the big reptilian front legs digging wildly into a pile of brush at the water's edge. Sticks and mud and little rocks were flying. The dragon looked like a cat in a hurry, and then something besides mud was being hurled into the air: soggy wallets, hats, necklaces, wet handkerchiefs, then eyeglasses and muddy photos—and many, many keys.

"What the hell," Richard blurted out, oblivious to decorum by this time. Abruptly the dragon stopped. It slowly raised its head and looked directly at Richard, a small shiny object in its mouth. The tail whipped back and forth several times and the little girl stepped backwards, a look of profound disappointment now making her eyelids flutter and her head wag sadly at Richard.

She watched the dragon as its pupils widened, fixed hungrily on the trembling figure of the man, and it stretched open a dripping mouth. "Was there something you should have told us, Richard," she said wearily. "Something you left out?" She turned to face Lake Overstreet. "Did you ever do anything wrong to someone called... uh... Phyllis, Richard? Because I think you have. It must have been something very, very wrong."

And as she walked away, she muttered in her little girl voice, "Anyway, bad enough to make a good meal...."

What They Don't Tell You About the AARP

"They don't look very comfortable."

"Comfortable? Jesus, they'll never be able to get up!" said my husband.

"It's got to be some kind of dementia," I said.

We watched the two old people shift from some kind of monkey squat and pitch forward onto all fours.

"I don't think they're supposed to be in there," I said, shaking my head toward the animal pen. "Do you think we should call somebody? This is too weird."

We were at the outdoor museum, an underfunded operation on the city's outskirts where a couple of eagles spit their feathers out over their shoulders, two otters adorably slithered in a murky pool, and a variety of other Noah's Ark refugees wandered aimlessly through the underbrush. Cleverer ones feigned sleep at the first whoop of anybody under six.

"For Christ's sake! Look what they're doin'!" my husband suddenly sputtered. The two old people, one, a woman wearing size 16 pedal pushers, and the man, delicately built with wasted muscles and large joints, had hobbled on their hands and feet to a little clearing.

"Maybe they're ex-gymnasts," I giggled.

My husband was leaning out over the metal railing where an attached sign saying, 'North American Grey Wolf—Currently on Loan to the Jacksonville Zoo', shifted in the breeze. These two were grey alright, but—.

"Oh my God…."

"George, oh, Jesus! Is he mounting her?"

The old woman's forearms were in the dirt, her bottom tilted up, and her wrinkled wattle bouncing as the old man rhythmically pushed his Bermuda shorts toward her pedal pushers.

"Mommy, is that Mr. Crocker?" A little head wearing a pink crash helmet knocked into my hip. Soon a mother pushing a stroller and a father shoving along a trike appeared from the Snake Pavilion.

"I think they're playing leap frog, Mommy."

The old man had dropped back onto his haunches, obviously winded, but was squinting in our direction as if searching for something he recognized.

"Look at that!" muttered my husband.

Now the old lady had happily toppled onto her back and was arching back and forth in the dirt, causing little dust storms to form around her grey curls and plaid shirt.

"I guess they don't smoke," I said, shaking my head with a smile.

"Hey, Mr. Crocker!" yelled the tyke at my side.

The old man focused on our viewing platform, and the woman smiled and sat up.

"Well, hello, Daisy," she said, brushing away some twigs from her backside and slowly getting to her feet. "I didn't know you and the family were coming today."

"Yeah, or you'd have worn your tasseled bikini!" hissed my husband.

George was one year from retirement, but everybody commented on how conservative he'd grown in the last year. Election to Senior Elder of our Mt. Olive Methodist Church hadn't helped. And lately he'd even been suggesting we give up our evening cocktail, saying it wasn't "seemly" for folks soon to be on Social Security to get tipsy. I'd snapped that, "If we can't do it now, when can we?" But that had only led to his leaving the Bible open on my pillow with little pieces of toilet paper marking scripture having to do with Sodom and Gomorrah and women following the examples of their husbands.

"How ya doin', Mr. Crocker, Mrs. Crocker?" The child's father had hoisted her onto his shoulders and was waving down at the pair. "See you're havin' a good time!"

"Yeah, Randy," the old man called up in an elderly chirp. "We a play'n wolves, today," and he turned to Mrs. Crocker, giving her a croaky howl, then leaned in and to her laughing delight, licked her twice right across the face.

"Oh my god," said George again, turning in disbelief.

"Well, you two sure know how to live!" called Randy. "Just be careful when the real wolf comes back." Randy's wife waved and helped the little girl back onto her trike. "See ya later…"

With happy nods, the Crockers then squatted down and went back to nibbling mites off of each other's necks. I had to get George home.

**

I had a hair appointment the next morning and left George busily scrubbing at the shower grout with an old toothbrush.

"That seems so pointless," I'd said. "It's old grout in an old shower. It'll never come clean."

But George said that you've got to do things right. Slipshod was how I'd been cleaning the shower for too long, and somebody had to tighten up around here.

We hadn't had cocktails for a few weeks now, and I thought George could use one. But I didn't say anything. Instead, I asked if he'd like to meet me after my beauty appointment for lunch—get him out of the shower before he emptied the crevices of all the grout.

"Pick up a bottle of tonic at the store on your way," I'd called.

**

The restaurant was crowded, even for early eaters like us. I arrived first and had to sit in a booth with a fellow diner's shoulder practically touching my own. But George usually liked this place. If you ordered before 11:30, you got free soup.

Four people had just been seated to my right when George came striding through the restaurant to our table.

"You're never gonna' believe this," he gasped as he jerked the chair out and rammed himself against the table, taking down the ketchup and salt.

22

"May I take your order?" The waitress was smiling at the elderly foursome next to us. Each of them wore a little silver pin saying, "Thrushwood Adult Center."

"Remember Carl, that old guy who stands at the front of the supermarket handing out chips in cups or whatever product they're pushing that day?" asked George. "You remember the guy, he told me once he's retired Air Force, served last part of WWII... flyboy... old school. Well, Jesus, you'll never guess what I saw." George put his head in his hands.

"I'd like the bisque, please," said the lady next to me.

"Yes, Ma'am. And sir?"

"Tuna melt for me."

"Got it. Iced tea all around, folks?" The little quartet nodded happily and returned the waitress' smile. How darling, I thought, like on a double date.

"So I see this guy from behind," George was saying. "Looks normal. I'm not even thinking about it. Then I go up and ask for some peanut brittle, and Jesus! He turns around, and he's wearing lipstick! Bright pink! And... eye stuff... got these little sparkles on it! And he's got his hair in these little... spitty... what are they?"

"Spit curls?"

"Yeah, spit curls all over his forehead! Sweet Jesus!" George was shaking his head from side to side.

"I just said to him, "What the hell happened to you?"

"You said that, George?"

"Yeah, and then this son of a bitch flyboy says, 'I'm retired. I'm old. And I just felt like it.' Says he always wanted to be a woman, and now something just tells him to let himself go.... He just don't have the time to restrain himself...."

"My goodness," I said, wondering what it would feel like to switch sexes after sixty-four years as a woman. Wouldn't mind losing my sagging D cups, I decided.

The people next to us were laughing heartily over something, convulsing really.

"Well heck, why have tea?" one of them guffawed. "How about we just order some nice cold ones?" One of the men signaled the waitress who raised her eyebrows slightly, then smiled her OK with four fingers in the air.

"I'll bet you can't get the cracker with your tongue," one of the old ladies giggled, tossing an octagonal saltine into the other woman's bisque.

"Oh yes, I can," said the soup eater as she tucked her wrinkled arms behind her and plunged her chin into the pink slurry.

"What the…?" whispered George.

After a few seconds of slurping, she came up with the soggy little nugget between her teeth, glasses dipped in bisque, liquid dripping from her nose.

"That's my Betty!" said one of the men, pounding the table with laughter and handing her a napkin with pride.

"OK, Charlie," he went on, "Bets on you can't catch a tomato, a bacon bit, and…." Here, he dug into his salad. "And a hunk of avocado… *between your teeth*!"

George and I couldn't move.

"No problem, Gene! I'll catch 'em and raise you one! You catch ten grapes from Edith's salad… *with your eyes closed*… and I pay for the beers!"

"You're on!" The whole table whooped and clapped, their faces flushed and eyes watering with mirth.

The waitress was setting the beers down in front of the foursome just as the first tomato hit the man called Gene in the forehead. A rapid barrage of grapes followed, ricocheting off Charlie's teeth—well, probably dentures.

"Are these people nuts!" George stage-whispered to the waitress, frantically cocking his head toward the old folks' table as if he'd developed a racking twitch.

"Oh, they're just having fun." She smiled benevolently at the little group snorting with glee and now using both hands to pick missiles from their plates,

"Is it in my hair?!" laughed Edith.

"Not till now!" squealed Betty, grabbing a handful of Caesar and pitching it at her friend.

"Oh you kid!" someone yelled.

"How about this…" Gene tucked a plump grape down Betty's blouse. "Let's see if I can get it—*not using my hands!*"

"OK, that's it! This is intolerable!" shouted George, standing up. "You people are acting like… like children… like animals. You're disgusting!" He stood spittle-mouthed, glaring at the food-pocked seniors, who with delight draining from their faces, began to pull lettuce and bun from their hair.

"We didn't mean to disturb you, sir," said the one called Gene. "You see, none of us has a lot of time left, and it just feels good… to… to play. Good to be silly. Good to be an animal. Here he winked at Betty and made a little "grrrr" sound.

"It may feel good to you, *Sir*, but you look ridiculous, and you are *totally* inappropriate for your age!"

George shoved his chair back and headed toward the door. I was left pinned in my booth and only Gene's pulling the table aside allowed me to rise and gather my purse and gloves.

That's when we saw it. As I turned to leave, I noticed something dangling from the bottom of my bag. We all saw it. A long, thick, yellow piece of cheddar from Gene's tuna melt.

As we stared at the cheese, six inches swaying slowly back and forth like the pendulum of a clock, Time seemed to pause for a moment. And then as Time will, it picked up speed.

I pulled the cheese carefully from my purse, feeling its warmth give in to my finger and thumb. I rolled it around, noting the waxy fat, the delicious greasiness of the cheese, and how it spread to my other fingers and palm. Then wiping my hand on the front of my dress, I placed the yellow sphere on the back of my left hand and raised it to eye level.

I smiled over at the four diners as I called loudly across the restaurant. "George. Oh, George, dear!"

Having reached the door where he stood, arms crossed angrily across his chest, George lifted his scowl in my direction. Then, I let fly. With a powerful finger-flick, I sent the cheese bullet in a straight trajectory directly at the "Ask Me What's Wrong with Young People" lapel pin he'd lately taken to wearing. But cheese balls are unpredictable, and sometimes they just go high on their own….

Suddenly all around me I thought I heard the playground cheer. I felt the stomping of little feet, which turned out to be my own. And I pumped my hand over my head with a ridiculous feeling of freedom.

"Good shot, Honey!" Edith was patting me on the shoulder. "Oh, that's a zinger, a real zinger!"

I looked at the bobbing grey heads. Ripe dandelions nodding their approval in unison. Faces smeared with food. Charlie put his parched old hand on my shoulder, a knowing smile spreading across his face.

"Would I be right in assuming, young lady, that you too would like to come out to play? No boundaries, you know. No rules at all. You see, we fired the referee," he chuckled. "He was way too strict. And way, *way* too young."

A Fair Exchange

Red Italian dust danced in whirlwinds in the six inches above the road. Here and there miniature cyclones rose up, then blew away again as the sirocco whistled across the empty slopes of Franco's *podere*. Last year and the one before that, the crops had burned up in the desiccating heat. This year it simply had decided not to rain. For as far as the hills to the south, Franco Perelli knew that the land was parched and barren and that the people who had tried to make it flower, had become dried fodder too.

Franco's Tuscan farmlet, the one tended by four generations of young men who had so quickly become old, and their once voluptuous women who'd withered beneath motherhood's chores, was so spent now that even the animals had taken to sleeping as much as possible—unconsciousness seeming the only way to suppress the writhing of intestines that like the actual inhabitants of Franco's farm, had nothing to occupy themselves. The corn was gone. The husks were too. Water hauled to the rough dwelling on the head of his wife was only used for drinking—bathing was done the way pigs did it—simply rubbing dust against the parts that sweat.

Again today, with his hat pulled against the brow of his lowered head, Franco had nodded to his wife and set out on the road. It was better to keep his eyes down as he plodded toward the village. Better to see only his feet moving forward, one at a time, seeming to evaporate in the dust that then settled into his shoes and their leather cracks. Better than to observe each neighbor's land lifting into the wind across the countryside.

"A man's life," he thought, "What is it worth?" His wife had sold her hair to the traveler in the cart who carried a bag with braids of farm women from as far as Sovana. He would sell his blood to the medic today. Soldiers could use it more than he. He hoped they wouldn't spill it. But when you offer up parts of your body, your *self* for a few lire, what are you? Like a milk cow who spurts out white liquid? A chicken who hunches down and produces an egg? You are a product-producing factory. You are little better than the olive tree from which is shaken its hopes of survival. Your actual life only has the value of a cup of petrol which when burned away, ceases to exist at all.

Franco felt the sweat dripping from beneath his cap. He wasn't hot, he was simply enraged. Why was the life he'd been handed so different from the one lived by the man on the hill ahead of him. Madonna! What God would design a system so flawed that Franco should starve and sell off his body, while Argento Calibio, the man in the *fortezza* beyond, should find money descending daily into his blubbery lap? Why should he bathe in cool water, eat fattened meat, and barely lift a finger except to caress a youthful wife? This was wrong. All wrong. Franco felt sweat running from beneath his cap, not because of the heat, but because of rage. Because of injustice. Because of the insouciant nerve of a so-called God to favor one and destroy another. And with that, Franco threw back his head and blindly screamed into the swirling wind, "I want another life!"

Overcome, he fell to one knee in the road, his head buried in his hands, his sobs ricocheting across the empty landscape, perhaps rising up the fortress's ancient slope. And then he heard the gentle voice, as if lips were pressed to his ear, "What about an exchange?"

Argento Calibio, grandson of the last Duke of Portino, slammed his foot onto the brake of the elegant black Alpha Romeo, and pulled the hand brake too, just in case. Even though he was one of the first in the middle Tuscan *provincia* to actually own an automobile, it was still a bit of a mystery to him, and its power intimidated him as much as his wife's temper. Still, a man of his position had to have one, his grandfather had told him. Such things were needed to keep up the "art of appearance." Then he heard it again. He hadn't been sure when he'd stopped the car. The sound had come first when he'd turned the wheel of the massive machine, and for a moment, he thought he'd heard a tiny bleat, like something small and helpless might make. But then the Fiat often made unidentifiable noises, though they often sounded as if produced by a gigantic digestive system somewhere under the hood.

Argento got out of the car and immediately, he heard it once more. This time the lamb was whimpering—sheep's voices sounding nearly human. Its leg was wedged between the tire and the fender of the car, and the lamb was nearly upside down in the wheel well. "Ah, poor little boy.... We'll get you out!" Argento fell onto his back beside the animal and stretching beneath the car, he worked his hand around the contour of the entangled leg. He felt the warmth of a little hip, the soft fleece of its thigh, and as he murmured to the lamb, he realized the animal had relaxed, only an occasional sound of what seemed like relief slipping through its slitted lip.

It hadn't taken but a minute for Argento to manipulate the leg free. With his face near the offending tire and four sharp little hooves eager to be set free, Argento held onto the lamb carefully. But the animal was in no hurry to depart. Sitting with his back against the side of the car, his tailored suit powdered with dirt, Argento and the extracted lamb settled into each other, the lamb's head leaning back against the man's arm. Argento curved forward like a new parent who is mesmerized by a beautiful new baby.

When was the last time he had felt like this, he wondered? Hidden from the fortress and the olive grove's managers, cached in the shadows from his factory's accountants who had all but moved into offices on the grounds, obscured from his wife who had no doubt found something new to buy or voyage to take, even hidden from the youthful *contadina,* with the looks of a movie star and the brain of a rock... When was the last time Argento had felt as happy as here with this lamb in his arms and its pecorino smell permanently scenting his suit?

This is the way he had always wanted it, if he told the truth. Before he had become a man, he had argued with his father to be let to live in a different house—one of the small stone ones he could see from the fortezza's wall, the kind of places the family patriarch dismissed with a shrug. Yet Argento dreamt of having pigs and a few cows. There would be lots of little sheep. He would raise their food and some for himself and a wife one day. There would be peace and village holidays, and the people from the *poderes* would come and sing, and they would harvest their crops together. But instead, he now owned an automobile that often seemed to want to kill him, and in turn he often wanted to die.

Argento looked up, his eyes needing to refocus from the soft, green, serpentine eyes of the lamb toward the dusty road. There was a man walking slowly toward him, one of the farmers from nearby, he guessed. He thought he recognized him… F… something… Franco, maybe. Yes, it was Franco, a good man with a good wife, and a charming cottage made of the stones he'd probably collected from the fields, and roofed with straw grown on his own land. Argento watched him come into dark relief. The man's skin was bronze, golden and healthy, he thought. His clothes weren't new, but though worn, the man appeared proud and self-made. Yes, that was it. He had made himself. He owned his own life. With few complications, this man, Franco, had a life that Argento wanted. A house, a wife, animals, and crops. This is the life that God gave to those He blessed.

Then, as if the lamb had stretched up and nuzzled his ear with a secret whisper, Argento heard, "What about an exchange?"

Laughing at the way the wind could so cleverly form air into imagined words, Argento set the lamb onto its feet and watched as it bounced away, making little scallops in the dirt. With each pounce, as the animal rushed to join its peers, Argento wished that he were running to where the lamb was going, wished that he were never, ever coming back. And then he got back into the grumbling machine, took off the hand brake, put his foot on the accelerator, and more quickly than he knew a machine that size could move, the Fiat suddenly shot off the road, careened into a ditch, and almost immediately proved it didn't feel like going back to the *fortezza* either.

**

At first Franco wasn't sure what had happened. He had seen the powerful black automobile seemingly parked on the road from the fort, as large as a locomotive he'd thought, and in the next instant, he could only see its grill and headlights smoking from within a small ravine. He ran as quickly as he could toward the accident, unable to imagine what could have happened in the blink of an eye.

But just as he topped the ditch, something inside the car erupted with a tremendous explosion—sparks, streaks of fire, steel engine parts, and a smell that Franco remembered from his two years on the front lines in the war. Its concussion knocked him into the ditch as well, and nearly on top of the man who had been at the wheel. There he stayed, half conscious, dreaming the clouds overhead were undulating concubines, yet wondering if together, he and the man beside him would soon be burned alive.

But nothing happened. Smoke smoked, but real fire never appeared. Franco slowly turned his head toward the person beside him, while that person appeared to be examining the face of Franco. "You are lucky," said Argento Calibri, without moving. "You could have been killed."

"You were *almost* killed," said the farmer, looking at the disheveled man in the dirt beside him. "For me, it would have been better if I had."

"Better? Don't be crazy. I know where you live... your family, your little piece of paradise. You are lucky beyond measure."

Franco scoffed, shoving himself onto one bloodied elbow. "You live in an ancient family palace surrounded by servants, factories that supply you with your heart's desires, a young and healthy wife... all of the luck has flowed to you, sir, and none to

31

me." Without realizing it, he sarcastically added, "Give me your life for one year… I ask only that." He took Argento's dirty hand in his own and then repeated the words he had heard earlier in the day, "What about an exchange?"

Argento smiled, but before he could reply, the second explosion sent the two men flying into the field. This time they landed far from each other, and the servants from the *fortezza* now poured down the slope, bringing a stretcher for Argento and bandages should he need them. Two men from the fort's stable arrived with a horse cart to take Franco back to his dwelling. All remained the same. The privileged receive privileges. The others do not.

And yet, an exchange based upon a smile might still be an exchange.

**

Franco had taken particular care with his toilette this morning. The whole thing was nearly over. His fingers trembled with anticipation as he struggled with the cravat which he never had properly mastered tying. It must have been a sadistic courtier who devised the silky noose a century before. Layer upon layer just to get dressed—his servant standing there ready to help him on with his vest, then the jacket. Oh, and now, slave-like, he was kneeling before Franco buttoning the spats over his shoes. Why?

"Argento," said his wife, proceeding into his rooms as if she actually spent nights there. "I will need 30,000 lire for the green silk dress and cape I told you about and another 10,000 for the shoes." She looked about the room as if to sniff out something not in its place. "You obviously did not listen when I told you I would be in Rome for the week since you haven't given me enough for even one dinner at Galleto's or for the shopping I must do." She stood examining her ever-compounding figure in the glass. "Just leave the money on the credenza and don't forget that my new armoire will arrive before I return. One hundred and fifty thousand lire, if I'm not mistaken." She showed herself a last profile in the mirror, apparently admiring something that Franco could not see. Then she was gone, the morning poisoned, and not only by her French perfume.

He hadn't expected the wife to be such a disappointment. Not by any measure, when the transfer had occurred. But there was so much that he hadn't known then. A bumbling peasant is what he had been, albeit, an honest one. Unschooled, yes. Unkempt, it was true—but willing to work for his bread. And as he looked back, he had been brought joy by a loving wife and friendship from others like himself who, during good times and bad, found shreds of solace even within the misery. Misery it often was, but this…. This was a different kind of suffering. The kind that masquerades and tricks others into thinking you're happy in the benefited life. Franco had something to compare it with, and he knew the truth.

The knock on the door told Franco that his comptroller was waiting for him to sit down with the accountants. So far during this year, three times, Franco had met with them, attempted to follow their bees' drone of figures and read something in the myopic eyes wedged beneath eight bulging foreheads so loaded with facts. He guessed they were all brilliant, but whatever their financial acumen, it seemed that the factory was on the brink of closing, half of the family lands would need to be sold off, and the disrepair of the fortezza's outer wall would either bankrupt him or simply end by tumbling the bedrooms and the western turrets into the valley below.

Franco straightened his cravat and smiled to himself that he really didn't care. Today was the day he would resume his own life on his own farmlet and embrace a woman who knew how to bake a loaf of bread. It was the day that he would see this entire enterprise resume its natural order. He was a peasant born and a peasant he would die—now knowing which life held what he desired. One year to the day, and the exchange at last would end.

Franco had a light lunch with a fine Suove Classico, allowing himself to reflect that he had indeed enjoyed the excellent wines

Argento had been brought up on. He would miss those. So too would he remember the winter evenings when *prosciutto toscana* hams, aging even now in the cellars beneath the fort, would be brought up and shaved into salty ribbons of sheer heaven. Those were moments that he might miss from time to time. And yes, heated water in which to immerse himself, and a valet to scrub his back were pleasant surprises that he might remember when he returned to his cottage. But he would not regret relinquishing these indulgences. Within the hour, he would return them, even their memories. And he would go home.

It had been a good year in the Tuscan countryside for those who worked the fields. Even as industry had failed, the weather had smiled on the olive groves and acres of corn and wheat. Everywhere Franco looked as he was driven to his cottage, he saw life springing from soil that only a year before lay fallow and suffering. With the rain and the fair weather, animals now grazed on new shoots, gardens burst with vegetables, cisterns were filled from wells that gurgled beneath their buckets. He could barely wait to once again see Argento and conclude their experiment.

At first Franco thought the driver had made a mistake. He must have driven down a wrong path to a neighbor's property. The stone building that stood in the middle of a lush garden was certainly not his. Nor was the bonneted woman who rocked an infant beneath a tree. Intentionally, Franco had not passed near his house in the year of exchange. His intent was to know, to enjoy the gentrified life without a backward thought. But, in fact, there was something familiar about this place. The small barn—his barn—had expanded. Three stalls and a pen now. And it was filled with animals. No longer emptied of all but a few straggling chickens as when he'd left it, now the place sheltered two dozen pigs with an enclosure for sheep. Franco got out of the car and walked in a small circle in the yard, his head swinging back and forth as if he were looking at a picture book rendering of a farm, one from a fairy tale.

The woman came toward him, diffident and smiling shyly. "Good afternoon, sir. May I offer you welcome." Franco had to grip the edge of the car so as not to sweep his wife into his arms. He guessed she had had to begin caring for children to help with expenses. She would be one to do that.

"Good afternoon," he said, realizing that of course, his voice didn't sound like his own voice, nor could she have known that inside the clothes, inside his fleshy exterior, she was being gazed at by the loving eyes of her own husband. "A happy child you have there," he said, tugging lightly at the baby's toe.

"She was born three months ago," said his wife. "It is the first for my husband and me." Franco couldn't speak, only staring at the woman, then turning to lay his head against the car.

"Sir, are you well? There is a bench beneath this tree. Please sit down. Please. I will get my husband." She ran toward the cottage, and he felt himself start as her words called his name, and another man emerged from the house. Argento came toward Franco quickly at first, and then more slowly, the realization of whom he saw on the bench apparently causing him to come to a full stop. Yet, like a good peasant, he offered hospitality.

Argento's outstretched hand no longer had the soft pallor of a hand used to holding a pencil or the steering wheel of a fine car. Calloused and brown, like the rest of him, Argento was tempered steel, balanced, steady, and perhaps not to be challenged. "Are you well? May I offer you something to drink? Perhaps something from our kitchen?"

Franco glared up at him. *Our* kitchen? The one where *our* wife bakes the bread and *our* baby coos at her breast? "I do not need anything at this moment. But I will speak with you... privately. I believe you know why I have come."

Argento looked down on Franco, now sweating profusely into his cravat. "It seems that you have been counting the days... perhaps the minutes? You seem eager for a change. But I am

35

curious, has the year been what you had expected? The little luxuries, the fat wallet, a large house with many hands to serve you…. Has it all been to your liking?"

Franco heard the sarcasm in his voice. Again, he thought, the privileged knew the advantage over he who was without. Argento knew that this life, the one lived from the soil was the better of the two. Franco remembered the smile on Argento's face as they shook hands and sealed their agreement, knew now it was he who had been duped.

"The year is up," he said to the farmer. "I've come to take back my house and land and wife… and her baby. It is time for you to return in this car to your fort on the hill." But Argento only shook his head.

"No," he said simply. "I will not go. It is here as I have always dreamed. I work hard. I've bred the animals into a healthy herd. I felled the trees to make for us a new room. I have bought oxen, and plow the fields for myself and others who need my help. And even as I refuse you, I offer you gratitude for the life I now live."

"But it is not your life!" screamed Franco. "We agreed for only one year!" He advanced toward the resolute farmer, who held up a hand.

"Those were your words, Sir. I only smiled." Argento lifted his shoulders, sighed, and walked toward the house. Then turning to look back at Franco, he said, "We both wanted a different life. We were both dissatisfied with what we had. I may have wished to throw mine away… to die… yes, to let life go. But I did not ask for yours. You gave yours away to me… a gift without a receipt. And I have chosen to keep what you didn't value." With that, Argento entered his house and closed the door.

For a long time Franco sat on the bench beneath the tree looking out over what used to be his land, listening to animals that used to be his. He got up and went over to the barn, looking in at the rows of chicken cages, where here and there a hen would readjust and a feather float outward into the light. And then further, he came to the pigs' pens, their black and white backs creating monotonal puzzles as they lie like children after a game of tag.

"What a life," thought Franco bitterly. "Fed on greens, sleeping all day, foraging in the forest, fucking any other pig that strikes their fancy." He shook his head. "It's with one of them I should have made my agreement. With an honorable pig who would stand by his word when twelve months had passed…."

Then outside, the wind seemed to pick up, and in the barn, the pigs stirred and stood up. They sniffed at the straw and each other, and moved from one end of the pen to the other, restless, and aroused. "So what will you have, Hams?" asked Franco. "Who wants to exchange? Who wants to sit in a grand automobile, and sleep on a silk sheet, and shit in a pot, and live like a man? One year, mark my word. One only. And I will do nothing but sleep and eat, roll in the mud and scratch my ass. For Christ's sake, I need another life!"

The pigs shuffled this way and that, most moving away from the rail against which Franco was leaning. Except one. A medium-sized pig, not a very intelligent-looking one. But one with moxie. "I'll do it, Sir," said the pig politely. "You said for one year? All right, I'll take a chance. I will live your life, and you live mine for one year only." And with but one blink of its long-lashed eyes, the pig raised a hoof toward Franco, who shook it in gentlemanly agreement.

With the understanding complete, Franco suddenly found himself surrounded by pink snouts that wiggled against him and snorted happily, rubbed by wet nostrils that shoved his testicles in friendly welcome. Soon dinner would be served in the trough he guessed, then a nap, a routine he thought he could just get used to. Already the relief of never having to see an accountant again rolled over him. Maybe never having to change a wet baby wouldn't be that bad either. And then the sound of a very large truck interrupted the pleasant sensation of a hairy belly scratching against his own.

It was perhaps a serendipitous thing in the end that with his transmogrification into a swine, Franco had lost the ability to interpret the dark marks humans scratched together on paper and walls and which, when seeing them, led them to make strange vocal sounds. Really, Franco thought, "Sooey!" was the only human communication one would need to know here. Yet, there are certain things that can be missed.

For when the barn door was slid open and the men walked in, there in the yard stood a big white truck that glittered in the sunshine. Some of those dark marks had been scratched along the side of the truck whose doors now swung open wide. "DePasquale's Slaughter Services" a human might have read in bold red letters. And as the pigs marched up the ramp and into the cool recesses of the van, they all snorted in delight. This would be something new, they seemed to think, something better than the straw piles they had—a new life in exchange for the old. Franco was the last to enter. "Last one on, first one off," he smugly said to himself, catching sight of the pig in a black suit sitting quietly on the bench outside. And with only a glance of sympathy its way, as the doors swung shut, Franco was grateful that he was at least, cleverer than a pig.

LOST AND FOUND

Arnold and the Lady

The last of the leaves still hung on the trees, ten oaks whose withering foliage suggested spiteful old people, who just to be contrary, clung to their twigs until the raker below had cleared the lawn, and then released themselves, spiraling in all directions, taunting him and teasing him to make one more pass across the grass.

But Arnold was on to them. Next time he would grind their skinny remains with the lawnmower rather than rake them. Then he would just call Fall done. Sort of done the way he was, he figured. Already the damp cold of the North Florida winter was coming on. Along with it was the depressing knowledge that grass wouldn't need mowing, and leaves would have all been raked, and that from then until spring, all the good Lord would have for him to do was to pass the long, dark, afternoons walking the alleys of town, looking for jobs no one else wanted—and occasionally wondering what the people inside the big houses, the elderly, rich folks whose yards he kept half the year, did with their free time.

He was thinking these things, his head down, heavy shoulders rounded as he stuffed recalcitrant leaves into a plastic bag, when he thought he heard the call of a wren someplace out by the street. He didn't bother to look for a wren, but most wrens, smart wrens, would have made at least a hundred miles south by now, down to where the warm Gulf breezes kept freezes at bay.

Then the wren began to sing in words. "Oh, sir. Mister, excuse me." Arnold didn't bother to straighten up, but only glanced under the arm that held the rake. People didn't address him as "Mister," nor did they say, "Excuse me," when they wanted his attention. Not to him.

43

"Sorry, sir," the woman crooned. Arnold stood up this time, slowly taking off the dirty watch cap he wore over what he knew to be his nappy hair. He hadn't even bothered to pick it smooth this morning—nobody to remind him to brush his teeth, or make sure his nails were clean, or have a nice cup of coffee before he'd go off to work. Nobody wanting to get his attention like this nice-looking lady.

She was still speaking, when Arnold lowered the bulging bag of leaves, not noticing that half its contents were being reapplied to the lawn. "I know this seems strange, maybe," said the woman, "but I just wanted to tell you what a wonderful job you've done on this grass." She brushed back a swatch of thick, wheat-colored hair, glancing up and down the swell of lawn that now, leafless, set off the colonial brick of the house. "How long have you been at it?" she asked. And for a moment, Arnold had the feeling that she was off-balance. That the question had suddenly careened her off her intended course of a friendly, but irrelevant pleasantry. He had the feeling that he was being—regarded.

And he looked back at her—quickly, because when you were a guy like Arnold, instinctual decisions as to others' motivations were the difference between losing your grocery cart of personal belongings, or maybe scoring a half bottle of Beam. Even as he sputtered, "A lawn like this takes upward of a day," he saw that her forehead and nose were pink as the camellia petals scattered among his leaves. That she wore lipstick, even though it was morning. He saw that under the scarf wrapped around her neck, her breasts were full and had maybe only just begun to soften. He saw by the slight tilt of her head that she had succumbed to something more than the mundanity of a passerby, and with all of this knowledge, Arnold took a half step toward her.

She didn't step back. She watched him, evaluating too. Smiling, and with a little shiver, she looked down, then back at Arnold. He couldn't tell what this all meant. White folks' cues weren't like what the women who came by his uncle's house gave out. Not like the young girls who lingered around the 7-Eleven late at night. Besides, money had it that this forty-something woman was married to a guy who owned a big house, drove a big car, and if she wanted, had her pick of lots of hired help. He saw the flash of something big on her left hand.

"You look like a happy man," she said, letting her eyes settle on him. "You look like you've still got some of the little boy in you, one who could roll in these leaves of yours and just let the sunshine tickle your nose."

Arnold hadn't heard words like that before. *Do white women talk like that to grown white men? Was that out of some book? 'Tickle my nose with sunshine,' huh*? "I like my work, Ma'am. An' yes, I been known to roll in some leaves in my day." Arnold decided to play along with this white talk. The lady was nice, even though it made him nervous how it felt like she was stepping right up to some invisible line.

"You want to do it now?" she asked. The woman stood staring at him for a second, then with a quick glance up and down the shady street, she began undoing the scarf from around her neck. "Let's do it. Let's empty the bags and roll." Arnold stepped back, protectively dragging the half-filled plastic bag with him. "Not sure, Ma'am... Not sure that'd be a good idea." *Crazy comes in all colors* he thought. *What she done shot up?*

The woman stopped halfway up the incline and bent over one of the half-dozen black bags, her fingers already deep into the leaves. "You probably think I've lost my mind, don't you? What adult woman rolls in leaves on a neighbor's lawn? What woman is so lonely that she stops a stranger doing his job to... play... like a puppy in the grass? That's all that I wanted. Just a moment of old joy... the kind I can't feel anymore... where leaf mold goes up your nose, and little pieces go down your shirt, and you don't care about your hair, or who scolds you afterwards." She looked at Arnold, and he recognized the feeling of being willing to take a punch for just one minute of freedom, just one second when you don't cater to anybody, when you don't bite your tongue.

"Well, then, lady," he said, slowly smiling and reaching into his bag, the feeling of stepping off a tall building exhilarating him, "We is gonna roll in some leaves!" And with that, Arnold threw the contents of his bag into the wind. The woman squealed with delight as the dried particles attached themselves to her coat and hair. Then she took one of the sacks beside her and ran toward him, hurling five gallons of leaves toward his head. Arnold reciprocated, dumping another bag onto her back, while on her knees now, she whooped, "More, more! You'll never find me in this pile!" Without hesitating, she threw herself into the heaps of crunching foliage and began to roll down the rise. "Whoa!" she yelled. "I'm going faster than you can!" Arnold laid himself out flat on one of the empty black bags and shot down behind her, overtaking her leaf-covered body just as together they were abruptly stopped by the dry ditch at the bottom of the little hill.

"Are you hurt?" asked Arnold, realizing the lady wasn't making those happy sounds anymore. "You alright?" He watched as she slowly sat up, wiping leaves and dirt and tears from her pink face. She pulled her legs up tight against her chest, smelled the cloth that covered her legs, and smiled up at him. "Come here," she whispered. Then she pulled his head toward her and buried her face in his hair. "I smell apples, though there aren't apples here. I smell hot chestnuts and chocolate," she said, raising his face to hers. "And the chance of snow, and school vacation, and the promise of a sled. And kindness, here," she said. "That is real. The gift of understanding without asking questions, the gift of taking a chance. Thank you."

She stayed a moment in the leaves, letting her fingers play through the yellow and crimson kaleidoscope, as Arnold looked away, confused. Then she stood, offered him a hand up too, and with the kind of hug he remembered his grandmother used to give, the woman whispered, "You offered me what nobody has done in a long, long time. You offered me joy… and maybe you saved me." Then with a smile, she turned and walked on down the street, glancing back once with a little wave, and disappearing beyond a curve.

Arnold sank into the jumble of broken vegetation. He looked around at the leaves scattered across the grass, from different trees, in different shapes and shades, layered together in an organic slurry, and wondered if, like them, somehow the white lady's soul and his had gotten mingled. His, worn out and weary, hers, weeping and hurt, but that mixed together, the combination in these last leafy minutes had healed them both.

Arnold lay back down in the leaves, flat on his back staring up at a luminous sky. He felt like he could float up through the naked branches and across to Africa and back. He may only be good at raking, but he had had a white woman turn to him for comfort. Made her laugh, made her weep with joy, and that was something to hang on to. White or black, she had seen him for the person he thought he was, someone of value, not just the chore that got done. You don't get a chance to be a friend every day, he smiled, or to have somebody value what you've got to give. Arnold sighed and closed his eyes. He felt proud.

Then he heard a rustling in the leaves. He turned his head to see a beetle that beside him was attempting to climb a tiny pyramid made from a couple of stones piled one on another. Something that hadn't been there before. Raising himself on one elbow, Arnold saw that between the two stones was tucked a bill, a slightly wrinkled, but very real, grey-green, fifty-dollar note.

He stared at it for a long time, feeling the disappointment slowly spill down his cheeks. Well, what had he expected, really? There it was, his wages for her "experience," for his "friendship." The payoff for a service, like what he got for mowing a field or repotting a plant, the confirmation that whatever had happened on the hill had been a business transaction only. Fifty dollars, fifty bucks that served as the gloves white people wore so as not to

47

actually touch the help if you shook their hand. Fifty bucks to remind you to exit through the back door. No, this is where things landed, didn't they, on an autumn morning, on an uppity street. This is not the place where souls got traded.

Arnold stood up and looked down the street where the white lady had disappeared. Maybe she was crazy, he thought. Maybe it was him. Loneliness can get you that way sometimes. But so can invisibility. They both knew about that. Arnold picked up his rake and began working the scattered leaves into mounds again, crackling volcano shapes that tried to slither back into the grass. He thought to himself, as he pulled them into position, of winter apples and roasted nuts. Of a time when he'd wanted a sled, and a grandmother's hug. Today, someone had given him these—when she'd touched his hair and shared her sadness. That was the currency friends dealt in.

Arnold gathered up his leaves and put them all back into their bags, leaving the fifty for the beetle at the bottom of the hill. It really wasn't meant for him. And with a last look around the pristine yard, instead, he shoved a red leaf into his pocket, the only compensation he would need, the only reminder of a day he traded in something better than money. The day he exercised his freedom as a friend, and very definitely, not the hired help.

Merry Christmas from George

If somebody had been watching her from across the street, they wouldn't have seen the little girl, the one whose eyes were wide and whose chilly red nose seemed to stretch for the smell of caramel, whose lips were already wet with the anticipation of the warm, sticky, candy-coated apple.

Instead, they would have observed an old lady shuffling through the parking lot, wrapped in somebody's discarded Lakers jacket, a black knit cap unraveling about her ears, and with arthritic fingers curled around the handle of the grocery cart she called home. The woman made her way methodically toward the food truck where energetic volunteers raising money for a Christmas trip to Disney were dipping bright red apples on a stick into the lustrous, sweet, caramel lava. She couldn't remember the last time she'd had such an apple. Only that it was in the Happy Time. The time before she'd grown old. And all of it—a step back there—now here, for the price of a dollar. Her fingers fluttered into her pocket for the last one she had.

Then he was beside her. What was he, six? Dirty-faced. Hair home cut and long. Dressed too lightly for the winter night, teeth unbrushed, fingernails bitten. He stared at the apples, watching the blonde-haired mothers plunging the rosy fruit beneath the caramel's surface, then twirling them onto the waxed paper, just the other side of a glass pane. Well, the old lady knew what they would taste like. That memory would never leave, she guessed. Maybe her teeth wouldn't take the strain of the first bite anyway. She shrugged a resigned sigh of relinquishment, and tapping the child on the shoulder, pressed her dollar into his dirty hand.

The child looked up. He knew all about money. He knew you'd better hand over any you found to your dad, 'cause if you didn't, a

49

backhand or worse was sure to replace the crumpled paper or silver coins you'd tried hard to hide. But the apples were so close, and so warm, and he'd never had one before. He stood trying to decide if there was time to eat such a rare pleasure before his father came out of the store with his twelve-pack—when something hit him from behind. The shove had sent him sprawling face forward onto the pavement, a little scarecrow with arms and legs in four directions.

The teenagers were laughing as they ran by. One leered at the boy, wagging the dollar he'd jerked from the child's hand. "Sucker!" the teen shouted, then disappeared with his friend into the parking lot while righteously enraged vigilante mothers punched 911 into their Smartphones with caramel-sticky fingers.

With hoodies pulled close, the teens hardly had time get a couple of joints lit before the sirens were echoing in the distance. Spilling out of the unlocked car they'd found in the parking lot, they tried to utter some dramatic, gangster-like curses, but all that came out were little panicky whelps delivered in voices that only recently had begun to break. With one or two thoughts about what Mama might have in store if they were hauled home by a cop, they snuffed out the poorly-rolled dope, and made a run toward the Walmart with its big neon grin and the Salvation Army ringer standing by the door.

Looking left and right, and assessing the nearness of a police appearance, each boy made an angelic show of digging into his pocket and casting something into the kettle before disappearing into the big store. But in fact, all that landed in the black pot were two disintegrating joints and a little boy's dollar bill.

The Salvation Army volunteer only kept his bell clanging to stay warm. Times were hard and almost nobody was contributing. In fact, those smartass teens were the first in the last hour. If times weren't so bad, he never would be doing this job. After all, he'd been manager at the gas station. Hell, if times weren't this hard, he'd never dream of dipping into the black pot a couple of times a night to tuck a five, or a rare ten-dollar bill into his sleeve. But what he pulled out tonight had a little added bonus—a barely smoked cigarette—yeah, M.J., that's what they'd called it back in Nam, and a 5-spot. Yeah, times were tough.

But he didn't see the crumpled dollar bill as it too tumbled out of the pot and skidded against the Walmart wall, adding itself to the bottle tops, filter tips, and dried leaves that huddled together like passengers waiting for a bus in the cold.

A man carrying a broom walked past the Salvation Army ringer. *Maintenance engineer* is the title they'd given him, but cleaning man is what he knew he was. Peering into dirty corners on a freezing night with a dustpan and broom was the last thing he wanted to be doing. Engineers didn't carry what he thought of as "kitchen equipment." But Walmart was a job, and his pretty little daughter needed to be fed, and by god, a man could take pride in anything he did—that's what the Good Book told him. Thank you, Jesus. And as if by magic, or holy ordinance, the little dollar bill in the corner released itself with leaves and butts into his pan. He looked at it a long time. Was this a sign that things were going to get better? He picked it out of the pile, straightened and dusted it off, and glancing at the cheerful blonde ladies down by the caramel apple truck, knew just what he'd do with this God-delivered gift.

A half hour later, his wife showed up in the old Ford, their sleepy daughter pulled from her bed to come pick her father up from work. Normally, he'd plant a light kiss on the little girl's head before they headed home. But tonight, he opened the door and lifted her out of the car. She looked around, rubbed her eyes, sniffing the air like a baby hound, searching for the source of the warm and sweet aroma that filled the air. He led his daughter up to the apple stand, picking out the reddest and juiciest apple to get a caramel coat. Then he put the dollar into the hand of a wearily grinning mother, and in return, she put the beautiful apple into his daughter's tiny hand.

They both looked with admiration at the glorious treat. The brilliant red of the apple shown out from below the slowly cascading caramel, and the little girl said it was too pretty to eat. But her father said it was for her and that apples were meant to be eaten. Still, she paused.

Then the child let go of her father's hand, and walked primly into the shadows at the side of the building. He saw her disappear around the corner of an old grocery cart before he caught up with her—before he realized that the grocery cart contained a bag of old clothes, and a blanket, and a pair of sneakers. And that an old woman in a Lakers jacket seated beside the cart was now holding the apple.

"I wanted to give you a Christmas present," the little girl was saying. "I know my Daddy will give me lots, but maybe you don't have a daddy anymore…." And she patted the old woman on the knee and ran back toward her father and the car.

Just then a gust of wind swept around the Walmart's wall, and lifted the blonde bobs of the Disney-bound mothers who happily counted their proceeds, and packed away their apples. Then without anyone seeing it, one wrinkled bill began to erratically flutter atop their stack of dollars. Then it caught a bit of wind, and suddenly lifted upward and over their little kitchen. Twisting slowly in the air, it hovered above the ladies and the black Salvation Army pot. It blew near the cleaning man, and the little girl in the arms of her father, and the old woman, who with tears glistening on her cheeks, ate an apple that seemed sent from heaven. The dollar bill danced in the air above them all, a tiny gymnast made of dirty paper. And then, as if called, as if he had only begun, George Washington made his way into the chilly night.

Take Your Shot

"I'm sorry, honey, I just can't make it. No, no... I'll just stretch out here in the office. Jesus, what a week. Yeah, presentation went alright. I'm sorry about it bein' Christmas Eve and all... but, Baby, I'm just shot...."

Julio watched him hang up. He hated walking in on calls like these. It wasn't the first time. When you emptied wastebaskets and ran dust mops across floors of a 20-story building, you were bound to pick up the detritus of lives—actually some pretty good lives, it seemed to him. But ones that people were often in the process of wadding up and tossing away.

Julio had to get down on both knees to pick up a half-crushed Starbuck's cup under a desk.

But now, the man's voice turned hoarse and low. "Shawnie, get those long legs over here, Baby."

"It's Schanda," she replied, as her six-inch heels clicked dutifully, and probably lucratively, toward the man.

Julio backed out from under the desk, shaking his head. "Whatever... *putana*."

Christmas Eve in Miami was not like the Christmases in the Yucatan. At home there was food—from mothers and grandmothers and dozens of *tias*. You danced, and you prayed, and you ate, and you all had little children on your laps. But not him. Not now.

"*Mi hijo*, my son," his father had said, "You are big, you are strong. You can be Olympian. You make famous one day. I cry, *si*... but you must go, *con Dios, mi hijo*. How do they say in America... 'give it a shot.'"

The elevator opened onto the 17th floor to a blast of salsa. Julio thought of "17" as the Cuban floor. Here the tall, smooth-skinned rich kids whose grandparents had come over in the '60s were raking it in in hedge funds and IT. He hated the way they looked at him, and he wondered how long a "Kevin Suarez" or "Blake Salazar" would last atop a heaving train in a desiccating desert.

"Ah, Chica… give it to me! Give it to me!" The Christmas party was at full throttle. Bulging breasts and bums that seemed shrink-wrapped in Lycra bounced to the beat, while men with oiled hair and pouting lips dabbed at white powder atop their lips. And in the center of the room a kind of human carousel made its way around the reception desk turned bar. "Tammy, get over here, we're doing shots! Two shots, one oyster, then two more shots! And we'll make 'um *long*!" The man shook his wrist up and down for emphasis.

Julio looked down. Just as for him, he guessed there would be no Christmas dinner for "Kevin" and "Tammy". They wouldn't even be standing in a couple of hours.

The men's room on "12" seemed empty. Paper towels littered the floor from missed hooks toward the wire basket. It felt almost peaceful here after "17." Julio began to silently pull on rubber gloves when he heard whispering.

"It's risky, I know… but the pay-off, buddy… the pay-off…." Julio could see the legs of two men standing in one of the stalls.

"Whoa… this is a long-shot, Jack. A lot of money…. But, hell… we both don't look that bad in orange…." There was a low, conspiratorial chuckle. "Let's take the shot." There was the sound of hands slapping shoulders, and Julio quickly backed out before the stall swung open.

After midnight the wind always rose on the lonely stretch of beach Julio had come to call home. Now, around three AM, the cumbia and salsa beats from the clubs had settled into a low thrum, and once or twice a homeboy's pistol shots could be heard in the distance. Around him, the sleeping bag had turned damp and cold.

Lying in the darkness, he thought of his father and his disappointed hopes for a good harvest. And of his mother, with her cluster of plastic flowers kneeling beside the graves of his three brothers. He pictured the girl he had loved, but who had fallen from the train coming north, and he imagined all the other lonely men, who like himself, lie alone on Christmas. All the people in Miami—no, all the people in the world—who innocently, naively, hopelessly, were "taking shots," "downing shots," "feeling shot," gambling on "long shots" that were, in the end, impossible.

Julio stretched out his hand, deep into the folds of the nylon cocoon, feeling for it—the cold metal—the one thing that could be sure.

He pushed himself out of the sleeping bag and walked toward the water, his fingers rubbing against the steel. There was peace here. A cessation of loneliness. An end to doubt.

He opened the collar of his shirt, and took a last look at the setting moon, luminescence wide now and stretched across the horizon. He had to do this, didn't he? What else was there for him?

Julio lifted the metal to his chin, and took a deep breath. Then he twirled himself in three small circles, planted his foot, and hurled the object into the air—putting the shot as hard and as far as he could. The iron ball arced higher and higher, far above the moon, across the sand, across the desert he had crossed, above the mountains of his homeland, faster than the train that had brought him here. And then it dropped. Like a period. A blatant statement of fact, into the sand of the beach, as far as he'd ever sent it.

Julio stood staring into the darkness, imagining what he might become, proud of who he already was. "Take your shot, *mi hijo,*" he seemed to hear from the waters that rolled up from the south, water that was filled with dreams. "Take your shot, my son... and make it a very long one!"

The Joy of Peeing In Your Pants

"You peed your pants!" In a cubicle in the ladies' room of the Blessed Bee Tea Room, Inez Stanley heard what seemed to be an elderly woman's voice—distressed, indignant, and talking to itself. It wasn't the first time Inez had heard women in toilets or showers at the gym talking out-loud to themselves. Women actually seemed to be doing it all the time, little commentaries on the quality of the toilet paper, how a pair of slacks was too tight, that the grocery store was next on their errands' list. Often there were embarrassing sighs of satisfaction with what must have been a particularly pleasant extrusion; other times the grunts made Inez flee the cubicle without even washing her own hands.

Today's *alto voce* exclamation was one of those times when Inez had flushed, jerked her skirt into place, and banged the cubicle door open as she exited the ladies' room, with her own exhaled, "Really!" as a terse rebuttal to the crude private thoughts of whomever was in the adjoining john.

That's how it had felt recently. Other people's lives drifting up and seeming to bang against hers. Like tormenting viruses that subtly strive to take over your DNA, make you think their thoughts, see things their way—like the woman today, who must have felt no shame in blurting outrageous things about what she'd done in her pants.

Or take last Sunday at church—and Inez didn't know how much longer she would be calling it *her* church. The new pastor was a married man with a couple of children. At least, that's what they'd known when he'd interviewed and gotten himself hired. But now at his first sermon before the whole congregation, he'd brought the family and sat them right up there in the front pew. Just the perfect positioning for him to show off little Bobby with the crop of blonde hair, Megan, a freckle-faced Natalie Wood look-alike, and Steve, a mustachioed hunk who it turns out is a raging queen who loves to cook shrimp. Yes, that's what the congregation had been treated to—information on Steve's virtuosic fingering of shrimp. Clever distraction to keep half the male worshippers from belting old Steve right then and there, and half of the woman to keep from belting the pastor in order to see if Steve couldn't be rehabilitated into going straight.

But instead, the church had raised up their hands and praised God for bringing diversity into their midst, and welcomed the new preacher's suggestion of many more "rainbow moments." That had been as much as Inez could stomach. She'd faked a coughing attack and dramatically gotten the hell out of the sanctuary.

Whatever happened to the way things had been? A time when you could have your private thoughts—say, about the extraordinary bulge in the lead baritone's trousers—and just keep them to yourself. Everybody just doesn't have the right to be or do whatever they want in public, Inez pronounced to herself. She was on her way back to her house where she lived alone with a cat she couldn't get near without getting scratched, and a parrot whose vocal apparatus she'd had surgically removed so that it could no longer repeat the obscenities it had learned at the pet store from young hooligans who thought it hilarious that a parrot could swear. Even the immigrant floor sweeper, trying to expand his vocabulary, had reenforced the curses. But that's how it was these days. People doing whatever they wanted, and others, like her, trying to put it all back together again—with some rules and decorum.

Inez took off her narrow-brimmed hat in front of the mirror in the foyer, then for a moment, put it back on her head. This time she tilted it to one side, the way the British royals do for funerals and horse races. She'd always thought those snobby, long-lipped women looked like tarts. She leaned in for a closer look, then pulled back, aware that an insouciant angle to a hat could make a woman with as many wrinkles as she had more pathetic than tart. She took off the hat, and slipped into her old flat shoes. Maybe just a moment in the garden would set her spirits straight. Get her mind off of human beings and onto… birds perhaps? A verdant tree? Even a squirrel. No, not a squirrel. Their little self-privileged, glassy eyes and tail shakes reminded her of Jean Meyer at the country club last summer. "Forget Jean Meyer," Inez told herself—even if none of the men ever would.

She eased herself onto the glider. From the patio she could barely hear the choking sounds the parrot made wanting her attention, and for now, the cat threat seemed to have abated with her upending a whole salmon can onto Angel's plate. All she wanted was to find a little peace and quiet, stare at a passing bee, and as she often did in solitary moments these days, to remember what her childhood and teen years had been like, to indulge herself in short-hop reveries to those golden days as a banker's daughter, a spoiled only child served by the Black help, and serenely secure that she knew where she was positioned in the world—and where the others fit in below.

Stretched out, shoes off, and with her eyes closed, Inez was reimagining her first cotillion, the one where she wore five crinoline petticoats, danced with Billy Chambers, and made everybody jealous when old Luther had shown up in the big car to carry her home. In her mind's eye, she was just stepping into the Lincoln, when reality slammed its door shut. Successfully blowing apart her daydream, from over the fence suddenly there came the opening snarl of a leaf blower as her neighbor's yard man revved up its engine. Not content to make a steady, albeit raucous drone, the blasts came in couplets, triads, sounds that swelled, then fell, punctuated with tiny staccato rhythms in between. Then just when one series of cacophonic roars had died and she thought the gardener might have lost interest and wandered away, they would be redoubled, as if he'd found a particularly egregious leaf pile that he intended to boot clear across the park.

"What in the hell…" Inez murmured under her breath. She pushed herself into a sitting position, and watched, as around the corner of the house a maelstrom of leaves and dirt swirled onto her patio. This was serious. This was personal intrusion of a higher sort. This should land somebody in jail, she mentally fumed. Inez leapt to her feet, now ready to confront whomever was behind the leaf blower and responsible for the affront to neighborhood tranquility and her own state of being. And then she felt it. A nail? Some thorn? Her soft foot had landed on something that was sending a fiery poker up her leg. Inez collapsed back down onto the swing. Only to find another poker thrust into her right hip. And then other pokers along her arm... but they were airborne! The swarm, kicked up by the detritus heaved heavenward by the blower, was white-heat pissed—words Inez would never have spoken, but was thinking now. She hopped and hobbled as fast as she could into the house where the cat sat snarling, and the parrot had begun a new round of gags.

Twenty minutes later, Inez, sitting on a cold pack and dabbed with calamine lotion, was driving north, away from the house. "What I need now is to not be here. Get away from all of them..." she said to herself. "The Sunday Schoolers and Libs at the church. Animals, whose next vacation spot is the pound. And oblivious yard men, vicious bees, and ladies who think an angled hat will bring happiness." Inez drove for a half hour, breathing deeply, and trying to focus on the passing fields filled with white cotton bolls, and the red barns where tractors would soon haul the harvest. This was more like it. Away from the city folk, and the country club, and the snotty pets—everything she was used to. Everything she found no longer really fit. It was as if she were wearing fashions from another age, mouthing opinions and thinking thoughts that somehow felt sour, but which had nourished her her whole life. She was tired of feeling annoyed, she began to realize, tired of carrying around judgments like rocks in her purse. If she were honest, Inez wasn't pleased with herself, either—wouldn't have chosen herself for a friend. And it occurred to her that even speeding out of town, she couldn't leave herself behind.

She pulled into an angled parking spot on the main street of the little town just north of hers. Strangely, as she opened the car door, even the air smelled different. She almost felt herself stepping into another dimension, a child's plastic toy city. Here people walked up and down the street carrying purchases, chatted on black iron benches, stopped to admire goods in stores that displayed books, and shoes, and kitchen wares. There was even a little place filled with handmade mirrors, where Inez did a double take, finding her own reflected face was flushed. And she was smiling. She strolled up and down the four streets of the town for an hour, buying homemade cheese and a little porcelain knife she didn't need, but which made her a participant in what felt like a charming holiday pantomime.

Just beyond the bookstore, she came upon a shadowed alleyway between two buildings. The owners had turned it into a leafy sanctum with brick pathways between trees that arced over umbrellas protecting each of the wrought iron tables. Filled with shade, a breeze played along the turn-of-the-century brick corridor, as red umbrellas gently tilted this way and that with friendly respirations.

If she had tried, Inez couldn't have held herself back. The courtyard was empty. Well past the lunch hour, only a few cardinals flitted through the trees, but the rest of the magical dining space was hers. She sat down, not caring if a waiter came to take her order or not. It would be sustenance enough just to drink in the quiet, the silence unadulterated by people and things. She thought she saw movement once. Something at the far end of the long outdoor hall. Yet she felt herself protected from intrusion, and only concentrated on how the breeze made the leaves move so gracefully. She must have sat there for a half hour. She could see a thin trail of people passing by on the sidewalk, but few turned their heads to peer into the blue-green shadows where she sat.

And then she heard the first spit. From the street side, the waitress was leading two large people into the alley way. Inez looked carefully at the intruders. The woman was wearing flipflops and what used to be called a muumuu, something that mid-century Hawaiian woman looked good in, she thought. The man, in a shirt that showed that the hair on his belly exceeded that on his head, seemed quiet and dull as he followed his grinning wife. Still, he managed another copious bolus of spittle into the geraniums, carefully wiping the exudate onto his fingertips which he then ran through his hair.

There were eight or ten tables, but the couple was seated directly beside Inez, who now sat upright with exasperation. They attempted to catch her eye, perhaps to apologize for their proximity, or to start a little noxious conversation. But Inez, pretending to reach for a menu that had been dropped on her own table, shifted her chair to present only her back to the pair. For a moment, she thought that perhaps people who spat into flower beds wouldn't have anything to say to each other—or worse, they would. Yet, she didn't want to leave. This was her spot, by God. And she felt an urge to defend it.

At first, the couple inspected the menu, murmuring about an arugula salad with avocados. Then after deciding on the T-bone steak, hash browns, sides of broccoli, a double order of hush puppies, honey butter, and the chocolate cream pie, the woman reminded the man that he had to call the doctor's office. "Better do it now," she'd said. "Gotta get that EKG sooner or later."

But he should have called earlier, it turned out. "We are busy helping other patients," the recording said in a loud, cloying voice. "Your call is important to us. You are 19th in the queue." Inez could feel her neck turn the color of the geraniums. "Hang up," she mentally ordered. But with his phone out, the man was now happily scrolling, ignoring the litany his wife was beginning to recall of each of the other memorable meals they had ever eaten—and what each of the others at their table had ever consumed.

"We are busy helping other patients. Your call is important to us. You are 18th in the queue." "You had the roast beef and beets… that were overcooked. I had the chicken piccata and French fries. Bob had fish and chips. Alice loved the cheese soup…" "Your call is important to us. You are 17th in the queue." "We'd never eaten sauerbraten, but you loved your ribs. I had red fish with spinach. Dad had tuna and black beans. Mom insisted on that turkey and gravy…" "You are still 17th in the freaking queue."

Inez could hear her heart beating in her ears. How could these oafs do this to her sacred space? To despoil it? To spill their banal smatherings into her personal perimeter? To not turn off their damned phone? And efforts to envision cotton fields and crimson barns were not helping.

Inez felt like she wanted to cry, and teetering in that space between desperate sorrow and blind hatred, she flicked on her own phone to counter "… is important to us. You are 15th in the queue." She hunted for a weapon. Something she could dip in a countering poison. Something to drive out the enemy to her tranquility. Something she guessed no overweight, self-righteous, country folk could stomach. In minutes, Inez's finger landed on just the station. She glanced over at the couple, now smearing honey butter on their second order of hush puppies, and she turned the volume to high. Then with the sensation of leaving lawfulness behind, she pushed Play. The last words from their table, "Your call is important to us…," were drowned out by Boosie BadAzz's pounding screams of misogyny. The hip-hop thundered from Inez's phone, bouncing off of the antique brick walls, and the floating red umbrellas. Even the hush puppies seemed to be throbbing with nastiness.

The pair turned toward the kempt matron behind them, eyes wide with the fear when a movie protagonist becomes possessed by Satan. The man stood up, as if to protect his wife, his phone still on, his not wanting to lose his place in the queue, while the woman simply covered her face with her napkin perhaps hoping to block out the sight of what was happening to Inez only feet away.

Looking back, she would have found it hard to explain what had felt like a pulsing fungus inching along her limbs. Inez had never actually heard hip-hop, only the name. Now, the thrusting, stabbing, repetitive beats of the music, filled with words she couldn't understand, awakened some inner version of herself that had lain dormant her whole life. Inez felt her head beginning to move forward and back, then her whole body arched and flexed, forcing her to her feet. Her head rolled side to side, her mouth moved in open vowels and sneers, delighting in obscenities spilling out in broken syllables that matched the beat. And she felt pure joy. Not the peace she thought she'd needed, but the liberation she'd never had.

Suddenly, from the shadows at the far end of the verdant alleyway, a dark man appeared. She thought she had seen movement there earlier, and now the anonymous observer made his appearance. He was no more than 30, dressed like the kitchen help, wearing a brilliant smile, and moving in time with the music and Inez. These were movements she had never seen. Forcing his pelvis forward, bobbing his head, pivoting, and squatting, she began to echo his steps—tentatively at first, but quickly letting herself go. Boosie BadAzz's pounding cadence, and perhaps first rumors of what was happening in the restaurant's outside eating space, were beginning to attract a small crowd on the sidewalk. And another crowd at the rear entrance near the kitchen, this one comprised of dark-skinned workers who knew their way around a hip-hop dance floor. Even as Inez felt people watching her, people passing judgement, exchanging glances of pity, or concern for the past-middle-aged woman who had gone nuts at the restaurant, had begun to gyrate to incomprehensibly foreign sounds, and with Black people at that, she felt both in and out of her body. As if she had died on the table and from someplace near the ceiling was watching the surgeon give up on the resuscitation. Inez felt she had a choice to make. She could slip back into the woman stung by bees, cursed by her cat, offended by others' sexual choices, and who pitied people who liked to eat, or she could let that Inez flatline, and instead hover here, dance here, try out a new way of being.

Just then, the hip-hop stopped. The owner of the restaurant was standing beside Inez's table with the still throbbing telephone in his hand. "Madam, this kind of thing is not permitted here. We have ordinances. You are disturbing the peace, and we will not countenance the kind of language you were using here on our premises." He turned to his kitchen staff, who stood wide-eyed before him and said, "Go in and collect your wages." The crowd at the sidewalk offered a small round of applause to the owner, who then turned to the large couple who still seemed to cower beneath one of the umbrellas. "And Professor and Mrs. Baldwin, as the conductor of our Jordanville Community Symphony, this display must have been most distressing to you. We therefore would like to make your meal complimentary, and to make an additional contribution to our annual orchestra pledge in recompense for your having been subjected to such a lapse in decorum." The conductor and his wife, nodded gracefully in thanks, and picking up their belongings quickly exited toward the sidewalk. "Your call is important to us. You are 8th in the queue," trailing behind then.

The owner announced that the restaurant was now closed, and the crowd quickly dispersed, headed out to buy floral arrangements for their studies, and bespoke earth sandals from the Shoe Boutique, leaving only Inez and a circle of five unemployed African American cooks in the courtyard. They stood looking at each other, each of them wondering if one of a different color would begin casting blame. For a moment, Inez felt the released facsimile of herself that floated overhead waver, felt a pull to reunite with the woman who loved Beethoven, and her garden club, and the supper dances where proper older gentlemen might just cop an arthritic feel.

But in the end, the choice was easy. Especially, when the man named Hoagie reached under his apron and pulled out his phone. Lil Wayne's rap began softly, then it built. And Inez let herself go with him, and with Hoagie, and the others. She had a lot to learn, she knew—about freedom, and judgements, and how to get down without looking silly. But one thing she had figured out already, that when you're having fun, abandoned to joy, truly in love with the moment, things can happen—and Inez almost giggled out loud, "I think I just peed my pants!"

Lift Every Hand

He wasn't even forty, yet most mornings Wayne could barely lift his head off the pillow. The usual wine-head throb he'd gotten used to in Paris was augmented these days by his new friend, Jack D., and a bong full of grass, or in the last weeks, sleek capsules that sent him into oblivion for an hour or two. Yet it wasn't enough to keep him dreamless. It wasn't enough to offer clarity to the day.

Wayne rolled on his back and fingered the spike of whiskers growing out of his chin and throat. He smelled the residual chemicals arising from beneath his arms, the build-up of three or four days of quiet rhabdomyolysis, a term he knew from his reporting on prisoners of war, who like him, were in the process of losing muscle tissue. And probably like him, losing their will to do anything about it.

He drew his knees up toward his chest, feeling his back stretch into a fetal curve that once would have been the precursor to another hour of sleep, but now only threatened to bring on a cramp. Wayne untorqued and shoved himself up into the position of an Edward Hopper silhouette, slumped and alone before an aging window. He pictured one of those characters, the one with the lonely woman in her slip, unclear if she were coming home or preparing to leave what seemed like a disconsolate hotel room in a friendless city. One very much like the one where he sat now.

Wayne stood up, weaving for a moment before propping his hand against the window jam and lifting the stiff, manila roll-up shade. The little tears in the fabric that tracked across its surface let in morning light without the preemptory glare of opened drapes. Besides, a rental like this wasn't about to hang anything that you'd have to clean. Across the street, he could see the elderly owner of what was now called a "boutique" grocery, happily trying to hang a little banner announcing the arrival of "Fresh Peaches." The old man teetered on an orange crate, his arms stretched high, groping toward a clothesline he used for such announcements. Wayne watched for a few minutes, a bystander's—or reporter's—instinct to watch for calamity overcoming his need to pee. Disappointed, he eventually shuffled toward the loo.

Standing over the icy commode, his mind converted the sound of cascading liquid into that of a waterfall in Kenya, where he'd camped with diamond smugglers, gotten laid by a couple of black prostitutes, and had his eyes opened to the ease with which millions could be skimmed off AID funds meant for the little beggars in the myriad slums. He knew that if he waited a few years, he might find himself screwing one in some Nairobi brothel, her skinny body never having partaken of the "high caloric" AID bounty. Wayne shook himself dry, wishing that the sound of falling water might have taken him somewhere else.

He dragged on some pants and a shirt, leaving socks and shoes for later. The hot plate would warm the place up a little, and while he waited for the water to heat enough to dissolve the instant coffee, he would try to organize the assignments that lay like paper yokes on the desk. Yokes, that according to their urgency and fee scales, Wayne would climb into and begin the slow drag for information— his resolute and disheartening accumulation of human misery for the "edification" of readers. This "purulent panoply" of what men do to one another, elegantly scribed so as to not leave the readership complaining, or an editor striking the description of a burned baby, a severed head, or manatee with the name of a president carved in its flank was Wayne's bread and butter. Indeed, he was nothing if not practical. He knew his commodity, knew where to go for understated outrage, knew the line over which one should not cross if you wanted to sell copy. Yet with his tiptoes right at the line, he had looked over enough of humanity's knack for the diabolical to know it made him sick.

Wayne glanced out of the window, the sun now rising behind the small brick stores. He could see a thread of trees in the distance, so dark it looked like a narrow slash of charcoal had been scrawled against the sky. Before he might mentally convert the strip of branches into the Czech forest where he had watched a cadre of government oppositionists dangle by their necks, Wayne downed his coffee and decided to go hiking.

Since he'd come home on leave, he hadn't gone more than a couple of miles away from the ignominy of the hotel and the anonymity it provided. The perfect blackout curtain he'd thought. Yet, it wasn't shrouding him from what he'd seen, scenes that like stitches of a knitted scarf where, when one thread is pulled, the whole garment, with all its horrors and mistakes, comes unraveling before you. Wayne was beginning to think there was no hope of his reknitting what his life had become. No way to make it whole again

He walked down the street toward the drugstore, knowing a headache pill would make a long forest walk more likely, only to find the sidewalk blocked by two men balancing themselves on a board stretched between two ladders. They were Hispanic he thought, giggling like children as they cavorted with paint buckets, waving dripping brushes in upraised hands in what looked like a soon-to-be disastrous highwire act. Wayne stopped for a moment, his reporter's mind on the alert, but there was nothing to see here. Just a couple of happy painters with only salsa on their minds. It felt odd to Wayne.

Outside the drugstore, two couples were chatting as they peered down into two black baby carriages. They were Hassidic Jews, delighted to have offspring, and no doubt planning for more. One of the men, his *payot* swinging back and forth from the sides of his head, reached in and lifted his baby high overhead. The other man did the same with his child. Pumping the babies up and down like weight lifters in a gym, the women giggled and the infants chortled, and the men struck goofy poses with their progeny held high, a tableau that stopped Wayne in his tracks.

As he walked out of the drug store, the city seemed to have decided it had overslept. Now the street was milling with people rushing to make it through yellow lights, to make it to important meetings, to stuff a breakfast sandwich into their briefcases, or their mouths. Wayne stopped to watch them. For him, he saw a threat on every corner, behind every wheel. Yet it appeared that each of the darting commuters was unaware of the terrors that danced like invisible partners beside them—catastrophes from climate erosion, economic gutting, insurrection by the very people who babysat their children, or the predators who mowed their lawns.

And then he heard a yell. Wayne looked across the street where protruding from a manhole in the road, were two dark hands. With eyes wide, Wayne crouched, awaiting the explosion or the implosion that surely would follow. Yet, the hands only stretched up to another man who was handing down a large piece of machinery. Their movements were in total synchrony. Helpers, helpmates, a coordinated hope of reaching some mechanical goal. Wayne stared at them. All it took for the next piece of equipment to arrive and be lowered into the hole, was for the man in the hole to raise his arms. As if that act alone drove the future outcome—the universe, in the shape of a colleague, happily complied.

Wayne was now on the outlook, though the thing that flitted across his mind was still unformed. He saw a little dog, its paws stretched high on the leg of a woman who now tenderly, stooped to pick him up. He saw a man running to catch a bus, arms flailing over his head, and a passenger reach out to give him a hand up.

He looked in the window of a shoe store where a woman stretched both gloved hands high to get the right box, when a tall fellow shopper accommodated her desire with a one-handed lift. Wayne didn't see many people actually asking for what they needed, yet somehow, what they needed was felt and wishes were being granted. With a little covert adjustment, he tried turning his own palm upward to see how it felt.

Wayne hadn't driven his car in the year he'd been abroad. It felt strange, as if anything could happen. Yet, once out of the city, the roads emptied, and soon he was passing wooded land that seemed perfumed and freshly coated in colored pastels. Ahead, the forest looked green and he could see large trees poking high against each other, like people in a crowd, shouldered tightly in either joy or competition. He pulled to the side of the road, realizing his headache had subsided, and that with the windows down, there was a kind of olfactory nourishment being delivered. Here the forest was thicker than before, and at first, it occurred to him that he would be entering it unarmed, no pistol, no cell phone backup, no tape recorder as a memorial of his last thought. Yet he felt the absolute necessity of plunging into the forest to experience whatever else waited for him there. He rubbed his hand across his face, remembering the thrill and anxiety when he'd gone to meet drug dealers in the deadly highlands of Guatemala. Yet this was different, he thought. And for a moment, he reflexively raised his hand.

Wayne had zigzagged for a mile and a half through the forest and the underbrush that slowed him. These trees were narrow, packed together like eager students, sunlight only here and there filtering below their canopy. He was at first on alert, but slowly he began to notice the foliage and the botanical mélange that lay all around him. Flowers in every color and curve. Vines that turned into thick tubes as they wound around trees that in turn, assisted them toward sunlight. Roots whose calligraphy formed a steady stairway for his route to higher ground. Wayne noticed how pretty blossoms on stalks seemed to smile up at the insects who tiptoed across their faces. How the grasses in between the trees looked like tiny goblins rising precociously from the earth. He wasn't exactly sure why he was here, but it was beautiful.

Shortly, as he came over a rise, the land opened wide. Now there were only large oaks—monarchs, kings. Wayne sensed them to be in a state of ecstasy. Each of the massive trunks spread roots across the soil, while overhead, exulting the morning, singing in choirs that only trees in rapture can voice, he saw their leaves tremble, their arms extended upward. Others would call them branches, but these were outstretched arms, lifted, draped in green, cupped toward heaven. As if at a revival beneath an expansive blue tent, their bodies lifted and limbs filled with silent praise, these trees waited. There was no clamoring, nor demands, or threats. They waited for the rain to come and waited for the sun to warm them. Waited for fire if it must come to stimulate new generations. They waited for their destiny with a kind of acceptance that this moment, this air, this earth was the perfect place to await their future.

Wayne watched them for a long, long time. He listened and he learned as he stood at the feet of the trees. He felt his fear begin to crack and to shed. He felt thoughts settle into a rhythm that was cadenced and slow, as if a breeze ruffled their surface, but would not stir the sadness and horrors he had known. And slowly he lifted his arms, little arms that wouldn't last 1000 years like the ones before him. Like an acolyte among wise men, Wayne took his place beside the trees, waiting for what would come, accepting what was offered, sure that it would be enough.

HOPEFUL, SWEET, and SCARED SPITLESS

The Other Side of the Parking Lot

I'm a local. I rarely go to the beach. But on a lazy Saturday, the primordial urge toward sun and water drives me there. And as they always do, somewhere in the parking lot, between street and sand, my inhibitions mysteriously evaporate in the steamy air. Rather like our turtle or gull counterparts, and with about the same concern for decorum, I too march toward the sea. There, at its edge, I establish my territorial kingdom on a faded terry cloth towel.

To my right, I notice a synchronous motion. Four old men stand in tightly stretched bathing suits. They aren't speaking, but from time to time rotate their aging backs sunward, lean forward to obtain a more direct hit by the ultraviolets, and then resume their silent broil. They remind me of cormorants with outstretched wings, drying or cooling, or maybe just liking the feel of sun on parts that are usually tucked away.

To my left, two teenaged girls languidly practice the feminine ritual of "the presentation of the bathing suit." As if in a ballet for tandem nymphs, off come the shorts, then a reconnoiter right and left. Then off with the T-shirts, followed by a gaze left and right. Finally, in unison, they gather up their curls, form exploding buns atop their heads, and in a synchronized pas de deux featuring smearing suntan lotion along their thin, white limbs, they slowly sink into the blazing sand, no doubt basking in mental applause.

Toward the water, a covey of gulls is being raised by hand-clapping children who run back and forth, alternately delighted or terrified by the swoop of the red-mouthed birds. Birds screaming, children screaming, racing far from usually restrictive mothers, who this time, only raise drowsy heads to evaluate the tonal quality of the squeals, readjust their Ray-Bans, and drift back to drowsy thoughts.

Here, nobody cares if your ice cream melts down your chest, if there's sand in your eyebrows, or if your cleavage—fore or aft—is showing, at least not until the parking lot. Here you can be loud, provocative, sloppy fat, or voyeuristic. You can talk to strangers, roll on the ground, throw things, or let your salt-stiffened hair stand out like a sawgrass palm. Somehow, here, steps from the civilization which stratifies and sometimes stultifies us, there exists an exuberant intimacy—us with each other, with the water and the earth, and all its living beings.

I've decided to come to the beach more often. I like these creatures who groom each other, pull stickers out of each other's feet, and cradle sleepy offspring in their sunburnt arms. I like the ying-yang of getting gritty, then washing clean; of building a beautiful sand castle, then kicking it into powder; and of old people hugging each other in the sunshine and whispering a kiss of promise. I've learned a secret about the beach—one tourists and travelers have known all along—there's a lot more fun on the waterside of the parking lot than you'd ever know from the street.

Pandemic: Month Eleven

Today I did what I did yesterday, but I did it slower. I cleverly elongated the time it took to walk from the kitchen to the cat's box, where I even more languidly bent to scrape rounded pellets into a plastic bag.

I washed my face in divisions, upper, middle, and lower strata, using up minutes that were overflow from an hour's nap I had tacked onto the too short night.

Counting the steps, I reentered the kitchen, pausing to regard the rain, to examine the stains on the deck, the yellow leaves of a stunted hibiscus, a row of untrimmed trees which the pandemic had set free to grow unfettered and ignored.

I speak to no one, though there is another in the house. And no one speaks to me. I presume the other's route through rooms and corridors is, like a rat's labyrinth, well-trodden, with turns at prescribed corners, and lights flicked on and off with an automaton's certainty. I smell the remains of the other's habitation—an egg, I think, and see a stain of coffee—a reminder that another hour can be checked off, and perhaps another if I too decide to eat.

The air is cold and the light blue from the refrigerator, a place for observing the residue of this week's evening hours. Withered carrots, a chicken piece and a half, the thickening milk, a baggie of something green. With a retrospective flash, I remember other meals, ones steeped in conversation, laughter with wine, animated stories of the season's trip to Italy, or even an especially large fish someone caught in a northern lake. And all of it now assigned to some long-term memory bank where there also reside the lyrical words of André Gide, or Rupert Brooke's poetry, or the photo of my father after he fell off the roof.

But for now, I take out a piece of bread. I cut it in half, hoping to prolong the creative process involved in butter and a glaze of jam. I take out another slice because to fill my hour, I must build in additional minutes with careful mastication. I have done this yesterday. This same, exact progression. Extract the bread, make the toast, then the butter and scrim of gelatinous peach. Bite, chew, swallow, clean up crumbs, observe the interior of the refrigerator again as I position each item back in its original frosty footprint. I can do this in my sleep. I am sleeping.

But today, on the counter, something different has happened. Disturbing at first. Something which causes me to move faster than I had planned. Yet a diversion which sends what is perhaps a thrill of rebellion across my shoulders—a flash against the physical rubric of my hours.

Only one piece of toast has appeared. The other, swallowed into the silver machine, thrusts from deep within the toaster what appears to be the blackened summit of a miniature mountain that is now lodged within the deepest crevasse of the device. This will take ingenuity to extract. It will need logic, and must be based upon my years of experience in the kitchen and, frankly, in life, to remove this finger-size piece of toast. I feel myself flush with the excitement of the task. It may take 15, possibly 20 minutes of concentration— of exquisite absorption. A project. Something to write about on the pages that have insisted on their blankness for months now. As I peer deep into the toaster, I pull from the drawer, a very pointed, very metallic steak knife, perfect for spiking the tiny morsel and hauling it to freedom.

Then from somewhere on the circuit made by the other in the house, comes a voice as angry and sharp as the knife must appear to the toast. "Don't touch that machine with the knife!" The Presence looms behind me and then removes the utensil from my hand. Exasperated snorts of disapproval made only by parents who would dislocate a child's arm in an act of traffic safety emanate from his shaking head. "You've got to unplug the toaster, for god's sake."

And I realize this will turn out even better than I'd thought. Better than *he* could have guessed. I yell back at him to "not treat me like a child." He shouts at me that I "should know better." He unplugs and inverts the toaster. He shakes it and finds some magic drawer to pull out the remaining lump of crumbs. He mutters. I am sarcastic. Our voices run high. We put our hands on our hips, our feet wide apart, ninjas or jousters sprung into action, our adrenals swelling with indignation and the interruption of boredom. And I find him very attractive. And he loves the way my cheeks have flushed. And singed crust is on the floor. And the cat misses the litter box. And outside the trees are growing and growing

And I may lose the bread again tomorrow.

Marina Brown

The Sweetness of Red Cabbage

I went home twice last week. Well, not exactly home, that would be impossible. The house I'm thinking about is 2000 miles and 40 years away. Other people sleep in its bedrooms and listen to the creaks of its floors. They watch from its windows and hopefully weave memories within.

But I did go home. To the real one. The one that, when you're six, is big, and colorful, and noisy, and constantly filled with sensation. It's a home that seems to exist, like an unwritten book, inside me. I can turn the pages and find whatever I need, any moment—and anyone. I can linger long, or just peek in and the people there acquiesce to my wishes. If only their faces didn't drift into the fuzzy margins—blurry and escaping, evaporating like twilight.

But last week was different. My husband and I had happened upon a tiny German café. A few tables, fewer patrons, but *gemutlich*—warm, cozy. Charmed by the rotund waiter, we'd asked him to bring us whatever he felt we would enjoy. First came a cold lager, followed by a questionable *blutzup*. Then proudly, he produced a crusty schnitzel, and in a cloud of steam, a huge side dish of *rote kohl*. Rote kohl—red cabbage. I placed the cabbage in my mouth and tasted its thick, soury-sweetness. Then I stopped chewing and held it for a moment against my palate, the warm, pleasant essence of red cabbage mingling with my own essence. Rote kohl. My German mother's rote kohl.

Her hands flashed before me, grating the cabbage. I watched her smile and she told me to be careful as I measured the vinegar. I could see her clearly. Black curly hair, flushed pink cheeks, and the little mole on her upper lip. I chewed slowly now, the warm cabbage soft and giving. Mother had made us all eat cabbage on New Year's Day to ensure money all year long. But tonight, money was irrelevant. With each bite I seemed to actually internalize a moment shared with my mother and I was truly home.

**

My week hurtled along. Errands, job, shopping, chores, now a race to week's end. One final business meeting to go—and I was late. To my chagrin, a detour had landed me at a train crossing just as the gates were going down. Looking up from my watch, I saw an aging diesel engine chugging slowly between the flashing lights. I stared. An engineer was sitting profiled in the cab, his left arm lying along the engine as if on the neck of a favorite filly. He wore a thick grey glove and even a traditional cap. Our eyes met. And I was home once more. A reflex, a conditioned response—I raised my hand, and leaning far out of the window, I waved—hard. I could hear my father's voice, "Wave at the engineer, Sweetie!" I felt his strong fingers lift me into his lap. He pulled back the corner of my bonnet to better see my face, and I kissed him in excitement, the smell of his aftershave circling me with joy and safety.

The engineer of the diesel looked at me carefully as the train moved by. Maybe all mature women in business suits didn't wave as energetically as I had. He couldn't have seen the chubby child in the blue snowsuit or her father's grin, but with a little nod, he waved a dignified, very professional railroad man's greeting. Home included someone just like him.

My husband had smiled when I'd talked about my mother's cabbage. He'd laughed out loud when I told him about the engineer. "I don't remember a thing before high school," he'd shrugged. His half grin and return to his book told me he considered living in the here and now a much more laudable attribute than my sorties into a misty retro-life. And yet, what I lived, I owned. What I saw, I possessed. What I remember, is mine.

I looked at my husband. Contemporary, up-to-date, a man of action. He felt me eyeing him and looking up, indulgently shook his head. Then with a little preoccupied smile, drifted back to his black, white, weighted, and measured reading—his internal life organized, solution-filled. I sensed a mutual pang of pity spring up between us. So much of his life I saw as missing. So many stories, sensations, revelations—so much lost that he didn't retrieve. He, of course, was puzzled by my wistful nods to the past and forays there.

I leaned down and glanced at the old cookbook laying in my lap—open to "Red Cabbage." There was a friendly stain on the page. Rote kohl and my mother. A train's whistle and Dad. Me linked to them, mysteriously and powerfully. My past. Me. Like a recessive trait that shows up at the oddest times, my past and its actors will always be there, waiting for me, surprising me, coloring my actions and my attitudes. And whether he knows it or not—my husband joined that worthy entourage a long time ago.

Stage Fright in the Time of COVID

One day, the man from Papua took my hand in his. He examined it, the articulating tracery of its vessels irrigating apparently unhealthy white flesh. His long fingernail followed a swollen blood way, perhaps thinking of a future meal. Yet, all he did was pat my hand with his dark one, smiling a different menu choice.

And I felt no fear.

One day, I climbed into a car with two Rasta men, their ashen dreads like monk's cowls in silhouette. Into the island's mountains we drove, high above help, wet in tropical sweat, a sick cat, a solitary woman, and two ganja Nightingales, who would take me to a doctor to heal my pet and not take a penny for their trouble.

And I felt no fear.

One day, deep brown eyes smiled into blue ones, her face as painted as mine. Admiring each other's feminine wiles, she taught hers to me. With liquified plants and powered hues and a sip from the calf blood-filled gourd, she made me into an African beauty, fit for a beating from an amorous lover, perhaps a third or fourth-taken wife.

And I felt no fear.

Today—I stood on the woodland path, its split my choice of the lake, or the upland road where in the sun, trees in full fountain, their arches turned rigid and ribbed, became woody spigots, watering the earth in green.

The morning's respiration still lying across the water hid life I did not know beneath. The hill above sequestered grouse and fungi, a turkey obliviated in shadow as brown as the snake who may wish to taste my toe. They breathed quietly there. They offered no position on my preemptory appearance. The grouse pecked. The fungus grew. The turkey preened. And the snake slithered a little sine wave through the leaves.

And today I felt fear.

New fear. Lonely fear that made me flee these pastries of life, these sweets of feather and skin.

I had learned it from within my house, where locked doors, and television sets, poison in plastic bottles, thick cloth that blurs my words and eats my smile have laid turns of fear across my volition.

A harmless understudy in the wings now, an impotent actor, stage-frightened, under-scripted, and not even made-up, I turn back upon the path I've walked before, still in rehearsal, not ready for a comeback, hiding from an audience I cannot see.

The Physics of Nations

I've noticed that humankind seems to operate according to the laws of nature and physics. Events, good or bad, like bodies with mass, seem to attract each other. A vacuum of ignorance gets filled with no matter what floats by.

And as in nature, things happen fast. Just as cells divide from one to two in an instant, and overnight a soft pink gum sports a hard-edged tooth, so too do nations spin. Today we are this, and tomorrow we are that. Reality shifts on the strength of a penciled oval—or perhaps we have simply awakened.

Why didn't we see it? This event. This vote. This eruption that has changed so much. Things aren't, until they are, of course. Yes, there may be rumors and hints; other events compounding to spark a pundit's "trends" or a sage's prognostication. But until they've happened, they aren't yet. They're not real. The viewpoint of another isn't ours, and therefore not to be believed. It couldn't happen. Not in my reality.

So, I asked a Roman who once ruled the world. And a Spanish duke mourning his armada. I checked with Queen Victoria, and a king of the Aztec nation, and even a Portuguese whose colonies could not be found. Like residents of an old folks' home, they sit in a circle, rheumy eyes searching the ceiling, motes of empires drifting by. When was power lost? Did you try to guard it? You were once so strong and proud—your ideals so grand. What the hell happened to you?

The sagging jowls begin to move, and I hear the jumble of words they repeat in a blended fugue: "It was their fault." "Only we

85

had the answers." "Somebody cheated." "There were conspiracies." "The rabble stole our power." "God shifted sides."

Then, one by one, the old rulers closed their eyes, too tired to see how they and their empires fit into the physics of being. How as they had finished growing, aged and fallen into the shade of other more youthful nations, their time was coming to an end. Weakened by storms, branches of ideas withered. Unnourished by compassion, the empires squandered their meager ideals, and momentum ceased. And though inertia curtained reality, any passing microbe would have its way.

Like them, we didn't see it coming. Our Chinese-made athletic wear made us look strong. A yellowed Constitution made us seem noble. Our electronic devices made us believe we were smart. And yet, we had aged. We wouldn't say it, but we'd used up democracy. It had given way to the avariced architects of personal power—and indolence.

Like the snow that remains lovely until the last flake has melted, or the tree that stands not knowing it has died, or a resplendent leaf that does not believe it will fall, we progress, as do all things—bursting into life, thriving in our prime, relentlessly rolling to extinction.

Weakened and infected now, it won't be long. Some will be surprised—like the mother who detects the new tooth. Like the man who finds the cancer. But it was inevitable. Teeth appear. Nations die. It is the cycle of being. Things aren't, until they are, of course. But I'm sadly putting my bet on physics.

WHEN LIFE
IS NOT KIND

A Love Song

By day, the swirling patterns of carpet and embroidered silk layered the bed, a rich and confused chaos of fabric that engulfed the slim outline within. But by twilight, in the soft blue that seeped through the curtains, I could see more clearly the outline as it rose and fell, hovered in silence, then, with a rustle, readjusted and rose and fell again.

I knew that she preferred this time of day, when the noises of the living became preoccupied and quiet, and even the birds turned away. I knew that in the twilight, her eyes, white and wide open, would wander the shadows, finding texture and form.

The figure beneath the fabric stirred, and her head turned slowly as if a melody had begun. I knew that she was remembering.

**

Meilong's black hair lies damp along her neck. The steamy Vietnamese road is splashed with shadows. She is full of youth and doesn't want the dust of the path on her dress. It is white and clean, and she is filled with spring and the sound of a war gone silent.

Ahead she sees the old women and slows as she watches them stoop to gather stones from the road. Like gulls, the old women chatter and dart forward and back, each with a stone and a curse aimed for the clean white dress, at this girl who speaks Vietnamese but is an alien among them.

Born from a Black soldier and a local girl's shame and left to toddle alone in the streets of Saigon, Meilong was one day swept up by an elderly teacher and taken home to his wife to raise.

Mississippi-chocolate skin, wild black hair flying in little helixes around the high cheekbones and tilted eyes of Asia, her face

91

told too well of a night that her countrymen would not let her forget—a face an old man found perfect and beautiful.

**

She coughed in the deepening dusk, and from beneath the quilt, a frail arm extended toward a tiny radio, and with effort, switched it on. The crackling of a faraway station drifted fragments of Vietnamese music about her bed.

She curled close to the tiny machine, her head, bald, with tiny sores dotting her skin. She began to hum and the bones of her fingers were moving. She was remembering again.

**

The refugee camp in Thailand is bleak. Tents, or tin and paper shacks stretch for acres. Meilong and her elderly parents have lived here for four years. People come and go, but doctors doctor, and teachers teach, and slowly a community has evolved.

It is at the camp, in a tin building to which Meilong goes each day, that she has learned the ancient instrument of Vietnam. The *thu cam*, a tall, stringed, harp-like device, is filled with the throb of longing hearts. As Meilong plays and sings, her graying teachers, who know they will never return home, nod at this half-Asian, half-Black girl, and tell her that the soul of Saigon is in her voice and in her hands.

But others hate her for it. One night, as she sings for herself on a little rise overlooking the camp, sheltered with her harp in a thin stand of bamboo—she is raped. Cruelly and with the anger of the gift-less for the gifted, she is raped, and her fingers are broken. With the fury of one color for another unlike itself, she is beaten. Just as cruelly, they leave the *thu cam* untouched beside her, never to sing her song again.

**

In the quiet American town, the tiny man kneels before her. He is old, with a permanent smile and blinking eyes, which seem perpetually wishing to understand. He places his hand on her shoulder and offers her tea. In the near darkness I see her turn. Her eyes, white as moons, never leave his face. If he wants to understand, she is willing him to know—and yet, she cannot tell him.

A passionate bond unites the old teacher and his once beautiful, half-Black child. For her, the one remaining dream has been of this devoted father, to live long enough to care for him in his old age, as a child should do for her parent.

She feels humiliated by this illness and hates its shame. Yet it is the shame of others that she wears on her face and carries in her body, shame she has chosen to endure with grace.

With a Chinese herb, her father rubs her fingers, which often ache. The fingers are twisted and tight, but every night he tries to stretch them. Her eyes never leave his face. I once asked her if her father knew about the AIDS and how she had been infected, and she told me that one day she would tell him, but she believed on that day he would stop loving her.

Meilong's pain grew worse. She rarely slept and moaned softly when she did. The old man asked me the name of this illness that had entrapped his daughter, yet with discretion, I could not tell him.

But Meilong had heard his questions and whispered that, at last, the time had come. That evening, I watched from afar as she pulled herself up and into a kneeling posture before her father. I had never seen her so thin, so weak. Her body trembled beneath the gauze pajamas. Silhouetted in the dusk, he seemed a Buddha, distant and unknowable, she a penitent for whom redemption was impossible and only honor remained.

Slowly she bowed her head three times to the floor, and the old man leaned closer. Her voice came as a murmur, guttural, rhythmic, halting. She spoke until her strength had fled and the words were all used up.

When she was finished, the old man rose. He looked out at the trees, black, with the brittle chrome outline of the new moon, and then without a word or a touch he walked silently from the room. Meilong did not move. Finally, she pulled her arms about her head and wept.

A week passed. Meilong had drawn near death. Her breathing was rapid and she was conscious only from time to time. The old man stayed away. The tea had stopped and he no longer stroked her fingers. It seemed that she had been right; his love had been withdrawn, the shame too much even for this affectionate old man.

But on the day before she died, the door to the house had quietly opened. Softly, the musicians filed in. They bowed to the elder father, then went to Meilong, around whose tiny wrists they tied white prayer threads. They arranged themselves around her pallet and began to play.

The old man sat alone on a chair, eyes fixed on the ceiling. Plucked and bowed instruments, soft drums, jingling cymbals, they chanted in the voice of a faraway land.

Meilong's eyes opened. She might have believed herself in paradise. The fragile muscles of her face pulled into a smile, and she gazed from one musician to the next. These were her songs singing to her again. This was her father's gift—his gift of love, not withdrawn, but compounded.

Meilong reached weakly for her father's hand. Her eyes were hollow, but riveted upon his face in gratitude. Without looking at her, as the tears coursed down his wrinkled cheeks, the old man's hand stretched down to hers, and he held her little fingers. Slowly, he stroked them—gently, ever so gently, he stroked her little fingers.

Upon a Midnight Clear

It hadn't helped that it had started to rain—or maybe it was snow by now. On the back of the motorcycle, her helmet was pelted with specks of something wet and cold. Ten hours and 700 miles earlier it hadn't been much different—only drier.

"Who do you think you are... a couple of players? Gettin' it all for free?" the manager had yelled when they couldn't pay the bill.

"I'm runnin' a motel, not a shelter. Now get the hell out!" He'd slung their backpacks and a tiny cooler toward the dumpster.

For the next several hours they'd settled themselves into the warmth of the big metal garbage bin, finding a blessed package of dinner rolls and an old hoodie that incongruously read, "Virgin Airlines." It was something to snuggle against. But then the rain had started and the organic parts of their dumpster mattress had begun to sag, and they'd decided it was better to just be on the road.

He'd told her that by the time they hit the desert, the weather would clear up. He'd made it sound like Arizona was one big dune, ruddy in the sunshine and warm to the touch. She'd even pictured herself rolling down the big hips of piled sand, maybe building a sandy version of a snowman or stripping down to her underwear to get a tan. But as wetness seeped into the folds of her hoodie, she remembered what a liar he was. Always had been. There was the "I've got a good trade" speech, the one where he lorded it over the bartenders who stood vacant-eyed in the fragrance of the afternoon's stale beer.

"Yeah, I coulda been a cop. I coulda been in air conditionin'. But I got a trade that I can take anywhere and make a buck—a good buck. I'm a journeyman carpenter and don't nobody can take that away." Of course, most of it was a lie. He'd pounded a few nails onto a few roofs—and for the rest of it—well, at forty, cleaning tables in a roadside bar wasn't much of a profession.

But when you're pretty, sixteen, and on the prowl, and nobody much cares about your ID, a good-looking guy with a smooth line, some swagger and a vintage "hog" looks pretty good.

Good thing nobody ever looked real hard at that ID, she smiled to herself. She had a famous last name, for God's sake, related to some high muckety-muck. It'd never mattered to her. That long-ago rich guy was history, and as far as she was concerned, only good for getting out of a speeding ticket—if she was lucky.

Right now, all she wanted was a place to lie down. The wet snow had stopped and on the back of the bike it was suddenly brutally cold. Overhead, the desert sky extruded one pinpoint star that as it rose, grew oddly larger in the blackness.

She put her hand inside the leather jacket he had given her when she first climbed on his bike, and deep into the flannel of the Virgin jacket from the dumpster. Even now, nine months after they'd met, and eight months after she'd known, the perfect dome of her belly still surprised her when she touched it. He'd always told her it was safe, something about a vasectomy. But, oh well, what was done, was done. She'd known he was a liar, and it was probably her own fault.

But the baby was something else. Hard to think about it—but she would be a good mother—better than the one she'd had. She would raise this baby to be special. Someone people would respect. Maybe, she thought, maybe he would even be someone who would change the…

Then the front wheel of the bike hit the ice, and the star began to spiral, and after the crash, tiny pieces of chrome still floated in the night air, clattering to the desert floor like so many fragments of the firmament of Heaven.

And there came a quiet upon the land, except for the bleat of a sheep and the lowing of a cow, who wept silently in the darkness.

The Flower Box

It was the first of the week, and I was on my way to work, taking the shortcut under the highway, when I heard the faint clatter of Randolph's cart. It was a noise that always accompanied the old man when he approached—at least in the early days. Sometimes the rattles were drowned out by the other sounds around him—the white roar of the highway traffic, the occasional shriek of brakes, or the frustration of horns as commuters jockeyed for position on the overpass above. I had gotten used to seeing him, strange as he was. Looked forward to it, really. Randolph had that effect. I guess you could call it charisma. Randolph lived beneath the cacophony. He had the shopping cart, which he called his "vehicular transportation." And he had a box—a semi-solid refrigerator carton into which he would crawl each night, pull a permanently damp, pinkish blanket up to his chin and fall into the deep sleep of proud homeowners everywhere.

Randolph's box was between the cardboard cartons of Zack and Charles, two of his neighbors in this formerly dangerous amalgam of men consigned to life in the rough. But with the aesthetic of a good homeowners' association, they had all positioned empty tin cans in neat rows in front of their boxes to form a hobo's version of a white-picket fence. If life success was about having staked out a tiny patch of one's own terra firma, Randolph, Charles, and Zack were all achievers—and they wouldn't be anyplace else.

Randolph was rattling closer now, shoving the grocery cart piled high with clothes, an extra pair of sneakers, a bent-eared calendar, a discreetly covered roll of toilet paper, and a large black trash bag stuffed with what Randolph considered the contents of his "desk." Over it all he positioned his pink blanket, topping it off with a weathered poncho. He also, incongruously, carried a garden trowel that he was never without.

It was the first time I had seen him in two weeks. Randolph was frequently "not home" under the overpass. But if I were lucky, I might find him asleep beside a downtown fountain in the park, or tucked in the doorway of the Social Security office where he claimed he'd been so many times that a stop off there was like visiting friends.

But today, something was different. I could see it in the form his dark silhouette made as he pushed his cart over a curb toward his box. This time I couldn't see his head over the jostling mound of debris that formed his life.

I was worried. For hard as it was, holding his head up high was something Randolph had always managed to do.

That head and all that went with it was the first challenge that Randolph had faced, he'd once told me, and his body and its twisted limbs seemed but the rehearsal for all the other adversity that followed.

Randolph had been abandoned 68 years ago in a trash can near a church in downtown St. Louis. The orphanage that took over his care quickly discovered that several miracles would be needed if the permanently squalling Black baby boy were to survive. His bald head was too big; his tiny back disfigured; his tongue protruded; and at the end of a shriveled left leg was a clubbed foot that seemed only good for kicking. One nun used to tell him his leathery skin gave him a reptilian look. Certainly, this infant was not one that would be adopted. The sight of baby Randolph didn't command love.

But somehow, he earned it. He survived his first year, and then his second. Randolph didn't walk for another two. And when he did, his curved spine and clubfoot gave him the look of a scurrying crab, with long arms reaching out for things to hold on to and a large head tilted like a crustacean for a better view. But as time went on, most days would find Randolph scrambling with a purpose—heading for the garden behind the orphanage, the place where he thought he'd found heaven.

Old men like the orphanage groundskeeper, Mr. Puckett, are often about as lonely as—little Black boys whose heads overshadow their shoulders or whose voices resemble growling crickets. And it was amidst the rows of gladiolas and mums, lilacs, and roses that Mr. Puckett had planted in a burst of horticultural creativity, that the old man and the little twisted boy found each other. With his nose buried in the blossom of a yellow rose or on his knees pulling weeds from around the gladiolas, nobody could tell Randolph from any other little boy. And Mr. Puckett loved him. The old gardener liked nothing better than to see the joy in his little acolyte's face when, every Friday, he would reward Randolph with a fragrant bouquet to carry back to the dormitory's beige bleakness—and a squeeze around Randolph's shoulders that made the boy giggle and nuzzle the old man back.

As time went on, they enlarged the garden. With seed catalogs laid out before them, they sketched spots for vegetables and ground fruits. They put in a few flowering trees. When he was 11, Randolph even presented Mr. Puckett with a drawing of a pond and a little arched bridge that would be surrounded with bowers of jasmine and pink bougainvillea—and maybe even a little gazebo where Mr. Puckett, who was having a harder and harder time walking, could sit and watch the colors of the garden turn as the season changed. Those were the times that Randolph said he almost forgot that he still reminded people of an awkward crab, or that his head was too big, or that his skin was as bumpy as a lizard's.

He'd almost forgotten until the day Mr. Puckett died. And on that day, Randolph's real life resumed, and the idyll in the garden disappeared forever.

In those days, orphanages tried to support themselves. When children turned 12, most of them were pressed into real work for the community, or as they grew older, turned out as near-slaves to

99

locals who knew a good thing when they saw it. Randolph was a hard worker, the orphanage's sisters knew that. But most of the jobs as domestics or cleaning personnel needed to be filled by orphans who were—presentable. Randolph fit no bill that could make the facility money. And so, he began a life below the orphanage, stoking the steam furnaces with coal, cleaning out weeping pipes, and sorting through the garbage—a job that would last until in his 20s, someone remembered the black "gargoyle", as he was now dubbed, and that it was time for him to go.

The only things Randolph took with him the day he was turned out were a cardboard suitcase, a trowel Mr. Puckett had given him, and cuttings from some of his favorite plants—from the garden that had long since run to weeds with dreams scattered everywhere.

The years after that varied little. With no home or education, Randolph settled into the rut of those without resources or love. And the little gargoyle was an easy target. He couldn't fight back when he was beaten. He couldn't resist when a larger man would take his few possessions. He became a fixture from the street at shelters and cold weather repositories for the down and out and, as always, an object of derision by people only a rung or two higher on the downward ladder of despair. Yet somehow, Randolph grew into something else.

I remember the cold afternoon he told me about meeting a little old lady trying to rake the leaves from her front lawn. Randolph smiled a toothless grin as he described the chance meeting and pulled the pink blanket tighter around his shoulders. "I be just pushin' my cart along when this nice ole white lady, she just sat down on her front step and looked up at me like she know'd me her whole life. 'I be tired,' she say to me. And I say back to her, 'Well, don't mind if I hep you out do ya, Ma'am?' An she just poked this ole rake out at me and she say, 'Have a go at it, son.'" And Randolph laughed his crackly laugh. "This ole white lady, she called me 'son.'" And after that Randolph and the old lady became friends.

Although he never wanted to stray far from his box, Randolph became a fixture in the aging downtown neighborhood populated by elderly women and declining men. His "white Mama" introduced him to her friends, and soon Randolph was limping to the grocery for them, painting their fences, cutting their shrubs, and gratefully accepting their gifts of a sandwich or lemonade beneath the big magnolias or oaks discreetly far from the house. There had been a trace of the happiness he'd known with Mr. Puckett— working with his hands, often working in the soil. But if Randolph had had any illusions about the relationships with these elderly Southern folk, it was made clear to him one afternoon as he struggled behind his "white Mama," carrying a large potted plant for her veranda.

It had come from across the street in the sweet high-pitched drawl of another old lady, a woman who only the week before had given Randolph a fancy hand-me-down shirt, a gift he had treasured. "Well, what you got the little monkey doin' today, Wynette?" called out the woman from across the street. "I declare if he don't look like Toby the Chimp from the circus last year," she'd laughed. And then shockingly, his "Mama" had called back, "He may look like a chimp, but he ain't so smart." Both women had had a good laugh. And Randolph knew that his time with the white folks was at an end. He'd put the potted plant down in the middle of the sidewalk, and turned and walked back to his box, ignoring the angry calls that were now coming from both his "Mama" and her friend.

But he had his trowel and those two strong hands at the end of powerful arms. And he decided to make his own world, one that would be beautiful and never hurt him. For the next year, Randolph lugged dirt—stolen dirt, maybe—from parks and vacant lots. At night he claimed bedding plants of various colors, and made cuttings from trees and flowering plants that sprouted in a dozen glass jars near his box. And slowly, as spring came, the tiny hobo village beneath the highway began to burst with curving beds of blooms. A half-empty bag of rye grass had turned into a lush green carpet; petunias, impatiens, marigolds, and sunny daisies spilled over one another. And at night, Randolph and his neighbors, Zack and Charles, and the other residents of this cardboard town would sit facing the lawn illuminated with the pink glow of halogen, talking about themselves, their old dreams, and their new project—the vegetable garden that they all planned to share.

By the time they'd dug in the pumpkins and squash and had the rows laid out, Fall was in the air. It was then that Randolph had gotten the news from a clinic doctor I'd urged him to visit. The strange aching in his side hadn't been from clearing refuse from the plot where their vegetable garden would grow. It was a cancer that had also taken root.

Randolph had never wanted to go to the hospital. He'd been forced to for a few tests, but after that he resolutely declined. Instead, he was content to sit beside his box, facing the expansive garden that was now aflame in chrysanthemums and late roses. He never complained about the pain that carved deep furrows between his brows. Instead, he wondered what would happen to all his work when he was gone. Though his neighbors had promised to keep the weeds out and bring water for sprinkling, Randolph had his doubts. He'd always worried what the police would do if there were ever trouble beneath the highway. But since the garden had come to dominate the lives of those who lived there, there never seemed time for petty squabbling. Now Randolph hoped it was all safe in the hands of Zack and Charles.

During his last week, I visited the little man each day. He was in a great deal of pain, but refused medicine, or to leave his makeshift house. He had accepted a pillow and a warm white blanket, but Randolph only wanted beneath him the thin pallet of cardboard that he'd slept on since he was young. And, of course, his flowers.

Zack and Charles kept a kind of vigil. Each time they took a new turn sitting near Randolph's feet, they would bring in another floral offering, and each time Randolph would try to rise to admire the new blossom and tighten his gnarled old hand around his friends'.

And slowly, the garden moved. From outside to in, chrysanthemums, and peonies, clutches of roses, lavender bouquets, and a paint bucket filled with trumpeting orange lilies, the men of the village plucked their garden to give to their friend. And that was the way Randolph died, the refrigerator carton acting as both bed and bower, casket and mausoleum—the garden trowel and a daisy placed upon his chest as a cross.

They had had nothing, these men. Mistrusted and flung from society, they'd beaten each other with self-loathing and given up on the thinnest of their dreams. Until the little Black gargoyle had dreamed one for them—filled with fragrance and grace.

The Middle Years

The old woman looked up from the pile of clothes that spilled from her lap. Twisting her neck back and forth, she tried to rest her eyes by gazing at the rolling hills that lay beyond her stained and dusty village.

Her hair was sparse, but inched its way from under a scarf she'd wound around her head. As she pushed the grey hairs back, she quietly mourned the brown thickness that so long ago had made her a village beauty. "Beautiful," she'd been called, but one who was ruined.

That was many winters ago. Now in this time of starvation, hope of the few cents she would earn by mending other people's rags crooked her back forward and sent her swollen hands to work again. This life, like the ones promised, seemed only deception and lies—a dream really—a life she must have made up.

"Get up, you lazy bitch!" The wooden door through which light cut in wide shards, slammed open. She should have paid attention to his oncoming shadow.

"Where's the food! I been bustin' my ass all morning while you sit here in your little cave, all warm and cozy. An' what I got to show for it—a big zero. Damn taxes. Damn prices. Damn rich sons of bitches who only want "artisans from abroad" to build their goddamn fancy houses!"

The old man's voice trailed off as he slumped at the table and ran his fingers up and down the back of his neck. She could see his shoulder blades like triangles through his shirt, and tried to remember what compassion felt like. There had been a time.... There must have been a time when he had felt it for her.

"Where're the boys?" he asked as she sat the broth and bread in front of him. There were five of them, plus two daughters, who were now humbly, though thankfully, married.

She sighed. "Out... out as usual." The old woman knew the short rush of air across her face before the blow landed. The way a bird squats before it flies; the way a piper takes in air before he blows it out, she could always anticipate when her husband's hand would smash against her face.

"What's that supposed to mean! 'Out... as usual'! Who wouldn't go out, rather than being locked up with a crazy old whore and their half-wit brother! Or is the little genius himself out, conversing with kings again? Talking to animals? Making a fool of himself in the square and butting into everybody's business!"

The broth had been knocked to the floor, and she bent down to pick up fragments of bowl and bits of bread. The man now left, kicking over the chair and leaving the door shuddering on its hinges as he plunged into the street, perhaps to find his sons who were somewhere drinking, or sleeping, or wagering tomorrow's labor on a hope of today's gain.

The old woman didn't bother to get up, but slowly pushed herself over to the niche in the earthen wall where she went for solace when reality hurt more than a blow.

Feeling deep into the recess she pulled out a tiny box. Save for her husband's tools, it was the only metal they owned. She opened the lid slowly, already feeling her nostrils widen, and brought the box to her face. It was empty, but the smell of incense was strong; tiny bits of its powder must remain twirling as if a little snow storm raged inside, she thought. Meeting the air, the fragrance flowed from the box, into her hair, across her stinging cheek. It was a salve, as if air had become water and she was cleansed by memories, and promises, and illusions, and yes, perhaps by her own insanity.

For the rest of it, all of it was gone. The money, the expensive spices and perfume. At least that hadn't been a hallucination. It had fed them, even when the donkey was sold.

She heard the door creak and looked up to see not her husband, but the tiny lamb the farmer's wife two doors away had given her eldest son. It had gotten loose and was now nudging open the door and walking toward the salty smell of the spilled broth.

But instead of lapping at the liquid, the lamb walked straight to the old woman, and with a tiny hoof stuttering at her gown, laid its dark curly head in her lap. She stroked the little animal, who closed long-lashed eyes and seemed to drift to sleep. She must have as well.

And then it began. She could hear the voices outside, angry shouts, building and surly, not her husband's, nor those of her sons this time, but authoritative voices, voices of police. She stood up, gathering the sleeping lamb in her arms just as the door flew open. The sun glinted off of the metal of badges, of weapons, of flashing headgear. She stood staring at them, protecting the small animal as if it were it they wanted.

"Where is he?!" roared the commander. "He's no doubt been here!"

The old woman drew the scarf closer on her head. "My husband is out... he..."

"Not him, stupid woman. Your son! The crazy one. There are laws, you know. Crazy or not... there are laws!"

"My son... he...." She held the lamb tighter, but she felt it relax into her arms, at peace, even as the policeman shouted above her head.

"My son... You cannot take my son. Perhaps he is ill. And... there is a promise... a long-ago promise..."

The policeman and his cronies laughed and pounded each other on the back. "Of course, there is a promise," one managed to say. "We promise justice for treason; punishment for insurrection; death for crazy people who pretend to be God!"

With that, he reached forward and grabbed the lamb. "I'll just be taking this too!" he said with a long look at the woman.

"It belongs to my son!" she wept, trying to hold onto the tiny animal.

"Ah, that's rich," sneered the policeman, jerking away his prize. "The lamb of God. Well, when I eat each tasty morsel, maybe it'll have some magical powers! Huh? Make me a better man! Maybe it'll just wash away all my sins? Oh yeah, how about this? Why not all the sins of the world...."

Marina Brown

The White Swan

The forest at night is like treading inside a womb, thought Quy. This is how it is before we are born—warm, dripping, dark.

Yet, as her rubber sandals softly compressed the leaves, Quy knew that this was not a place of life. This was where spirits lingered far from home, where souls yearned to flee to a proper burial house, far from the crunch of bones and burst of bombs.

Quy walked quietly, her black hair tied tightly against the pull of vines and thorns. She no longer wore the conical hat of her village, but a bush hat now, pulled low on her face, hiding her eyes, making her anonymous in the forest, a thin, wet spirit herself.

The Central Highlands of Vietnam had been bled of its young. Fighting the French, toiling for the Vietminh, and now sent south as Viet Cong guerillas, generations of tough, wiry men and delicate girls were, like Quy, purveyors of an endless war.

But tonight—perhaps all of that would change. She inhaled the sweet composting fragrance of the forest, wondering if when she left this place, that scent would remain on her skin.

As she walked, Quy imagined how the narrator of one of the VC propaganda films would explain the strange existence she now led: '*Deep in the tunnel complex of Cu Chi, the vast warren of ant-like passages sheltering hundreds of guerillas, sixteen-year-old Quy nurses the sick, feeds the living, and makes bombs to kill Americans. Day disguises itself as night within the tunnels; while night is meant for a VC to turn himself into a snake or a tiger, prowl the forests, and trap his prey.*'

For the last month, Quy had rarely gone out of the tunnels. Bent at the waist, she, and scores of other peasant girls scrambled through the earthen corridors, dragged sacks of rice and metal, and like

108

insects, carried away the dead. Above, the American jets had seemed angrier. When the VC fought with bamboo sticks, the Americans threw fire. It seemed even the shaman could no longer make you invisible.

But only a few hours ago, with a boy's quickly whispered words, the twisting corridors had seemed to fill with a remembered scent of a blooming yellow apricot. Was it the sunshine she yearned for? The scent of blossoms in her hair? Perhaps escape smelled like flowers.

Quy settled her back against a tree while she waited. And as always when she was very quiet, images from the long-ago day on the hilltop came rolling back. The day she learned why she had been born—the day the puppies got away.

**

It was barely morning—before she and her father took the little dogs to market, when six-year-old Quy felt the swan. Felt it before she saw it. A cool shadow passed across her face, and she pulled wider the slit in the woven wall of her hut. Suddenly the light changed, as if the rush of a wing were scattering drops of sun across the forest's floor. Then the swan appeared. Its arcing wings embraced a current, each feather interlocked, long neck pointed south. Like an ivory arrow, the snow-white swan was going home. The little girl looked at her own skin, white-smooth like the beautiful bird's, she thought. So different from her mother's. She had seen men smoking cigars, and the brown, rough, parchment cover of those stinking sticks made her think of her mother's hands. Ten wrinkled cigars rolling dough and making morning pancakes.

Abruptly, the sleepy image of her mother squatting over the fire, weathered brown face squinting in concentration, was brought to life when she called Quy to breakfast. "I am an unworthy daughter," Quy said out loud, as she jumped to her feet and ran to gather water for her father's tea. But she lingered too long at the water urn. Was it her fault her little white fingers reminded her of albino fish playing in iridescent circles, or that they could splash the water into rainbows that hovered in the air like colored dew.

"Quy!" The girl jumped to her feet, scattering fanciful fish into the dirt. Her father's wispy beard and small muscular frame were still imposing as he stood over her. She examined him, looking closely for signs of displeasure, but instead he smiled and handed her one of the puppies. "Gather the others into the basket. We must go. Mothers will be shopping for the tastiest puppies even now," he said.

Quy rode atop the water buffalo. Swaying gently, the smooth black skin of the buffalo's back smelled like mushrooms, and Quy rubbed her nose against the rhythmic hump.

The puppies tittered and rearranged themselves over and over in the woven panniers draped across the buffalo's rump. The fact that they would be eaten didn't disturb her; even this buffalo might one day be sacrificed with spears and an ax to honor ancestors. These puppies would be honoring someone's stomach today.

The market was filled with noise by the time they arrived. Quy's father positioned her on a tiny mat with the baskets of dogs in front of her. He would return after examining a hoe he needed to buy. She was to demand 10 francs of a Vietnamese and 20 francs if a Frenchman wanted to buy a puppy for a pet. Quy nodded and placed one of her mother's large, woven conical hats on her head, feeling very proud to be left in charge.

But no sooner had her father disappeared in the warren of stalls, than an earsplitting sputter brought shouts in Quy's direction. With a final eruption, a shiny car so large it seemed one of its red-lacquered fenders could swallow Quy whole, came abruptly to a stop before her. As the occupants of the rolling palace began to step out, the shoppers surged forward.

A Frenchman stepped from behind the wheel. He had a thick beard and a fat red mouth that was shouting in anger. He was clearly furious at something. In any case, after conferring with an official from the market, she saw him set off into the crowd, arms waving and his face growing a deep purple.

But there was someone else in the car. It was her leg that Quy would remember. Even years later in the forests with bombs crashing above her, the vision of the French concubine's leg would always linger as it had at that moment. It was the purest white, as if the leg had been carved from ivory. Quy could see it was covered in silk, precious and untouchable. The child looked on and the woman stepped languidly onto the running board. The leg had only introduced her. Then came her pale arms, her milky neck, and against the creamy hue of her face, two little red lips that reminded Quy of coffee berries.

The woman held a tiny handbag and a small book. She looked around, tossing a curved helmet of golden hair. Quy heard her sigh, and felt sorry for the magical creature, but even more, she wanted to touch her. She wanted to know if her fingers too, were like albino fish. She wanted to run her own little hand along the arm of the woman—and she guessed it would be like touching a swan.

At that moment, a foot in the crowd kicked over the basket of puppies. Suddenly four little dogs were skittering into a labyrinth of legs. Quy cried out, people lunged for the fat little bodies, and the concubine involuntarily stepped back as shouts pointed the direction of the escape. Quy ran, distraught, but laughing, as she grabbed at the heels of the quickest dog, when suddenly, it leapt forward. As Quy fell onto her knees, she heard a startled, "Oh!" Looking up, she realized the puppy had jumped into the lap of the concubine, and Quy stared into the face of a surprised, giggling woman who seemed not an ivory statue, but a kind lady of blushing flesh and gentle manner.

The woman petted the little maverick for a moment, and then her attention settled on Quy. While the swan's morning passing had blocked the sun's rays, the concubine's gaze seemed to radiate warmth. "But you are beautiful!" the woman said to Quy, who knew a smattering of French. "You do not resemble the others here. What is your name, child?" Quy could barely speak, but she whispered her name as the concubine reached out her pale hand and cupped Quy's face.

"Look, my chérie," and the woman pulled Quy's little arm against her own, "You are as pale as I am! Perhaps we are sisters!" she laughed. Handing the puppy to someone nearby, the concubine took a writing pen from her handbag and began to write something in her book. When she was finished, she handed a page to Quy.

"This is a promise, my little Quy. Don't forget." Quy took the paper and was handed the puppy—and then its captured brothers all replaced in their baskets. When she turned back, the car was restarting, the bearded man still shouting behind the wheel. Soon only the receding profile of the concubine as it turned into silhouette was left.

The practical marketplace, however, had lost itself in novelty for only a time. Now the chickens were cackling, and the pigs were grunting, and all would resume as it had always been. However, one old man, perhaps a teacher, squatted beside her and asked to see the note. He smiled as he read the French words aloud to Quy. "One day, come south to Saigon, ma Chérie. You will be greatly admired for your beauty. A pale little swan like you will indeed find great success." The old man gently touched her arm and nodded in agreement.

"Protect your beauty from the sun," he said. "Protect it from the wishes of men. And one day, as the woman has written—in Saigon, the world will become yours." Quy didn't understand everything, but in that moment, she felt that a purpose had been laid before her. And that night as she dreamed, swans and albino fish played happily together in the warm waters of the Mekong far away to the South.

**

Somewhere in the distance, a bomb fell. A bomb did not fall alone, Quy knew. Others would follow. In Cu Chi's dark warren, the tunnels trembled as if responding to the pain of the earth far away.

Quy looked at the slim young man squatting beside her, his black pajamas stained and wet in the candle's light. Minh rarely whispered. But he was whispering now, so close that Quy felt his breath tickle her ear. A teenager like Quy, Minh was a painter. On other nights, he'd told her of red powders he could turn into sunsets and green dust his brush could make into leaves so real they would blow in the wind. Quy knew that with their VC comrades, Minh pounded American tank parts into land mines, armed camouflaged pits with nails and wires, and sometimes even shared his blood with wounded cadre through chicken veins and scavenged electrical cords. Yet, this thin man was not like them. Scratching at the earth with a stick, Minh could make rabbits and mountains and images of wild deer spring up from the dirt. When she told him of the paper note she carried in her pocket he had said only, "Yes, yes," and his eyes had looked very far away, toward the south. Quy remembered he had let his fingers shyly touch her own.

Now Minh's words spilled out. In the dim light, his eyes were wide as he told her quickly that the dream they both had dreamt separately was about to become real. "We shall go tonight, Quy. You will leave first—I will join you one hour later."

It was hot in the tunnel, the air outside turning to steam. Perspiration made their skin glow in the thin light, and for a moment, Minh imagined the translucent skin of the girl beside him had turned to alabaster. Perhaps one day he would sculpt her, he thought—far away from this place. His hand touched hers. They were chaste, these two. Believers in beauty; it was the only aphrodisiac they permitted themselves.

Quy had guessed that he was planning their escape. They would surely be shot if found out. But Minh had described the large Americans as kind to those carrying white scarves. They would be allowed to go to Saigon, he'd said, to safety, to the lake with softly-rowed boats—where maybe even love could grow. And she agreed with a slight nod of her head. The concubine had foretold her future. "We will fly like birds, to the south."

Quy had been waiting for nearly one hour in a hesitant rain just under the rise that was the patrol perimeter of the American base. Her eyes closed from time to time as she squatted on one wet haunch and then the other, listening to the sounds of the forest, awake with closed eyes or at moments, asleep with eyes open. And then Minh was beside her. Again, he whispered, but this time, his words came in a rush. The Americans were planning something bad tonight. Something dangerous was about to happen. They must hurry back to the tunnels; not even a white scarf would protect them.

"Hurry, little swan, hurry." he pleaded. She took his hand, and then the bombing began. The explosions didn't come first. Nor the whine of plummeting metal ripping through the trees. It was the shudder of earth, wavelike spasms violating the forest floor and rising up Quy's legs. Then came the sudden evacuation of air and sound, as if the whole sensory world were being swallowed. Quy took two steps. She saw herself running—but it was a dream.

The bomb burst open beside them. A radiance that enveloped everything, destroyed everything, illuminated the two tiny figures. Minh turned to look at Quy. Her eyes, round as sequins, glittered in the napalm's dance, and the whiteness of her face reflected the rupturing trees and burning clouds. Even their breath seemed on fire.

In a thunder of white phosphorus, her hand evaporated, and his eyes. The second bomb ate out the forest. Again and again, explosions filled the air. A third bomb erupted above their heads. Quy's black hair curled to powder. In a tornado of fire and greasy phosphorous, Minh's fingernails softened and slowly dripped to the forest floor.

The planes passed again and again in their hour of predawn exercise until at last, worn-out and empty, they grew tired of the game. The dawn raid gave way to an azure morning. The pilots departed, feeling hungry for breakfast.

The forest continued to erupt with exploding shrapnel and bursting trees, but slowly, it too subsided in a kind of sob. Pushing aside burning leaves and hot soil, the hidden cadre now crawled out of their maze to gaze at the forest. Seared and crackling, the canopy's blackened stumps jabbed helplessly at the sky. The soldiers walked about in silence, slapping at embers thrown up by their rubber sandals. There could be nothing living here, no one to repair with tape or wire or suture. Only a tiny movement in a crater drew their attention—perhaps just a shift of wind.

Impossibly, it was a hand that moved. It slowly stroked the dead animal beside it, an animal without skin, roasted red and wet.

"You will be my eyes beautiful Quy." came a broken voice. "Though I will not see you, your pale skin, like moonlight on a swan, will light my days." There was a pause and the cadre expected no more. Then more softly, "Soon we will fly to Saigon, to float on the lake, you beneath your parasol for all the city to admire." Flesh rolled in tiny scrolls about the man's face and chest. Where there were eyes, dark emptiness ran deep and red. Minh coughed, a hot, stinging cinder scraped at his throat. He held her wrist, imagining the soft white skin of her body that would one day wrap him like satin and soothe his blindness.

Imperceptibly, a breeze began to grow. Fallen cinders stirred on the forest floor. As if from a sigh, cool currents began to thread between the blackened trees.

Then it began. The stricken cadre looked up at what seemed to be transparent bits of rice paper, white, powdery, drifting in the air, falling along their arms and in their hair, as white as the skin of a swan—incandescent in flight, the spirals eddied down in goodbye. The pieces of flesh hovered in a tiny whirlwind over the darkened form of Minh until at last, the breeze freshening toward the South, the fragments rose—a promise to be kept on a bright day in May.

MAGICALLY REAL

Deep Dive at Lake Overstreet

It was late afternoon, no, later, thought Marion. It was nearly evening now and she was still at the Women's Club Buffet and Planning Session.

As usual, the food had been superb, half of it catered by Tallahassee's most upscale "ladies' luncheon" epicure, the other half proudly prepared by the members themselves and presented on family porcelain heroically saved 150 years ago from marauding Federal troops. It seemed that most of the plates were covered in whipped cream delicacies—just to emphasize that the ladies were secure in their wide floral dresses and didn't give a damn about their hips.

But what these 60 and 70-year-old former debutantes did care about was demonstrating to anyone who actually cared, just how fabulous a party they could throw while they raised a few hundred dollars for a charity that was usually selected by a pink fingernail landing arbitrarily on a spinning disc.

"Unfortunately, our fundraiser will necessitate our cleaning things up a bit," said Fostine, a tall woman with what looked like sculpted marshmallow hair. There were knowing looks and tittering agreement. "These two big ones are going to be *pickles* to get out," warned Trilby, staring at a photo with a smile that wrinkled already pleated skin. Everybody knew what she meant. *"Pickles"* equaled "goddamned hard."

"Well, I think the park maintenance people will welcome it," sniffed an ample woman from down the table. "Lake Overstreet has become overgrown with vines, and there's Spanish moss on everything. Those two or three outsized oaks are almost touching the water, for heaven's sake. I think they really do need to go. Get

119

them out of there and you'll actually be able to see our party lights. See where the neon sign points for you to go for cocktails." She delicately adjusted a bra strap through her sleeve. "We should even have them grade flat some of that land you can't even stand up on… certainly not with heels."

A younger woman, someone who had actually been to a university, not just a finishing school, said, "Those oaks are called century oaks. I believe they are protected…."

There was a wave of embarrassed laughter. Embarrassed for the neophyte, probably Northern-bred, who didn't understand priorities. And didn't have any relatives on the city council.

"It'll be alright, dear," said Fostine, patting her hand with the concerned look of someone who has just seen an incurable mole appear on a delicately rouged cheek. But the motherly solicitude abruptly turned to shock when the blonde shoved her chair back, looked up and down the table, and with the words, "Cutting them will be alright? I don't think so…" draped in the air, departed the Women's Club as if each woman may have an oak ax tucked beneath her chair.

"I'll go and see how she is," smiled Marion, shaking her head in disapproval, but in fact, grabbing her own purse and stiffly rushing toward the door. Was it the "neon sign?" Or the "grading?" She wasn't sure. She vividly recalled old house foundations near the lakeside—along with a few long-rotted clapboards beneath layers of humus. It seemed that many years before, there had been a clearing in the tobacco field that came right down to the lake. It was hard somehow for Marion to imagine bulldozers grooming this wild edge of Lake Overstreet into a sculpted socialite salon.

Everyone knew that people had lived here once upon a time. That this had been someone's home. Her nurse had told her so. Her "mammy," if she were truthful. Ruby May, a woman Marion had loved above all others. Ruby May, who was filled with stories about talking turtles, and tobacco leaves that turned into ball gowns, and even tales of ghosts. The old woman had told her there had been a community beside Lake Overstreet, one protected by the massive oaks the Ladies now wanted to grind to dust for the sake of some neon sparkle.

Marion glanced around the parking lot looking for the Northern college girl. But with a quick shrug, the outlander was dismissed, and Marion climbed into her lugubrious Olds and headed for the place that had begun to dance in her imagination. A place she could now recall as clearly as her childhood sandbox or the snowball bush she used to dance around until she was dizzy. So many lives she seemed to have lived since those days, pointless ones filled with hopes that hadn't materialized, rewards she'd prefer to void, important people, who, in the end—weren't. Yes, too many lives like the current one that was just accumulating days, too many days since the excursions with her mammy that had left her at peace in a way she hadn't found since.

Marion drove to Lake Overstreet, just to see, just to see if it was the way she remembered it when she and Ruby May used to trudge along hilly, muddy paths, and down to the water, to wait for mystery to well up and to listen for crawdads' call.

It had taken her longer than she'd thought to walk all the way in. The forest had grown up, it seemed, but there were still little landmarks. Ruby had had her sing them out like a boat pilot bringing in a barge, lodging them in her memory. There were the "three rocks hill," "the old fence pen," "cow path crossing." Names that Ruby must have remembered from her own youth when all of this land was used for farming, when the soil was turned, and the tobacco leaves harvested by tenant farmers who'd started out as slaves.

And then there it was, Lake Overstreet—wavering like a wash of opal through the trees, little flashes of blues and pinks, maybe a diamond's flash as the setting sun caught a ripple. Marion sat down, a log as long as her car inviting her. And for the first time in years, she was unaware of her arrhythmic heart, or the tinnitus in her ears, or the swelling of her manicured fingers that hadn't touched a tree's bark since she was 12.

She hadn't kept track of the hour. No one at home anymore to worry about her or even turn on a porch light if she were late. And god, how quickly night falls when you're outside and around you trees are trellising a kind of cocoon, a little room with walls of darkness for you to hide in, but which you guess may be invisible to creatures nearby who wonder why you're sitting in their house.

"Well, howdy do, Miss." Marion shrieked as she leapt to her feet. Behind her, the lake seemed a horizontal escalator with one wind-propelled striation following another. Even the sky, softly dusted with light from the city, was mobile, cloud banks imperceptibly turning from ruby to purple, and disappearing again into air.

"Sorry. I didn't mean to scare you, lady. I don't see folks here much, likely not after it get late."

Marion stood staring at the man, a black man, old, dressed in worn work clothes she thought, though it was dark. A straw hat he'd taken off, he held at his chest like a waiter anticipating an order. Yet his manner was as genteel as a cotillion coach would have instructed a gentleman to approach a lady, and as warm as had been Ruby May's when she had tucked little Marion into bed.

Marion stared at the man for a full minute, evaluating the level of danger, the distance to the top of the hill, and the fact that she felt absolutely no fear. "He could overwhelm me in a second, drag me into the bushes, or do it right here…" And yet, the murmurs of a bird in the underbrush, fireflies that themselves were becoming party lights, and a languid splash of something going for a swim, flooded her with an immense calm.

"What is your name?" she asked.

"I be Lacey, Ma'am. Born and reared right here. Yonder, near where they made that big cut for electric wires, that be my home site." He made a slight bow, incongruous, she thought for a man in overalls and work boots, but charming somehow still.

"Well, my name is Marion Dowd. I'm from near here too, but I don't get to the lake often." She glanced at him. "You say you still live here? I thought this was all pretty much park land."

Lacey moved his arm which caused her to start, but he finished with an Edwardian sweep to suggest she might like to sit down again.

"Not by day, Miss Marion. But in the shadows... just like it always be... in the shadows, that's where I stay."

Marion saw the last light of the night sky play across his face, his dark skin turning turquoise and sienna, a daub of vermillion hovering for a moment along his cheek. He must have been a handsome man in his youth, she thought, smiling to herself that many a white Southern woman had had such thoughts in their day.

"Would you like to see my house?"

Marion could have watched the hairs along her arms rise, if it weren't dark. "Never sit on a man's lap. Never, never, never go to a man's house... white man or otherwise." And certainly not in the dark, nor *in the woods*.

"I would, Lacey," she said. "I would indeed."

The trip up the eroded trail hadn't been easy. Rutted into inches-deep crevasses, Marion had stumbled several times, steadied by a strong dark hand that reached back just in time. She hadn't noticed the lantern Lacey carried until now, but in the distance, through the trees, she could see that there were other flickering lights silhouetting trees that turned golden green.

"Here we is, at my house," said Lacey, holding his lantern higher. "My wife and the young'uns all inside by now." Marion could see figures moving back and forth through the four-paned windows. A woman bending as if hunched over a fire; four... or did she count five... children darting here and there, dressed in rags, she thought, and a cat leaning into the crooked hand of an old woman who sat silent in a corner. The air was filled with the smell of burnt wood and food. "Miss Marion, welcome to my home," said

Lacey, opening the door. "Stay as long as you're able and share the blessings of our family."

As if the reel of an old movie had just snapped, all movement in the room abruptly ceased when Marion appeared in the doorway. Midstep, the children stared at her with mouths ajar. The wife straightened herself into a statue of shock. And the old woman's gnarled hand even stayed itself halfway down the cat's back. In her turn, Marion stared back. Seeming to appraise some unusual, medieval painting, she examined their expressions—fear, confusion, perplexity— emotions denoting what must be for them a surreal experience. "What in Jesus' name is a fancy white woman doing at our house at dinner time?" was frozen in their eyes.

"Thank you, Mr. Lacey," said Marion, stepping over the splintered threshold. "You are very kind to invite me." It took only seconds for the family to reanimate. With barely a glance at her husband, Mrs. Lacey pointed to an older child to set another plate, and to a younger one to retrieve some water from the well to give Miss Marion a drink. Meanwhile, the woman lifted a skillet of fried bread from the fireplace's iron grate and set it on the table to cool. "Take your places chillun. Blessin' time." Lacey pulled a low table in front of the old woman and tucked a cloth around her neck, then went to the head of the table.

The blessing was short, not delivered in the Old Testament oratory style Marion had heard from TV preachers, but rather a simple gratitude for work, requests for assistance to bear up under whatever life might bring, and a special thanks to the Creator for Marion's unlikely visit. And then everybody ate. After the bread, came little fried pieces of something meaty. Then boiled greens, freshly wilted. And a special treat, walnuts from a glass jar into which each child insisted they had cracked the most.

"Pull out that mouth harp, Thomas," said Lacey after the dishes had been taken from the table. "Fred, you get the strum-can." The girls of the family set up a kind of assembly line in front of two bowls of water, one to wash, one to rinse, and another child to dry the few dishes and put them on an open shelf. "You ever heard a little farm music, Miss Marion?" Lacey handed a pair of wooden spoons to Fred, and exchanged them for what appeared to be a kind of guitar made of a gasoline can, a board, and some long wires. Then he began to stamp his foot against the rough pine floor, and his leathery hands to pick out the rhythm of a tune.

Soon, Mrs. Lacey was clapping her hands, and around her, the girls were swaying back and forth, bobbing their heads, and prancing their skirts across their knees. "Ah ain't been down to Jer'slem town, done slept instead, done gone astray," "But now ah'm home, done changed my ways, an' now be singin' dem halleluyay."

The room was still hot from the fireplace, but everyone was moving to the music, sweating happily, stomping old shoes or bare feet, children twirling, singing at the top of their voices, Thomas turning out to be a harmonica virtuoso. Then Mrs. Lacey, unable to restrain herself, jumped up from her chair and reaching both hands out to Marion, pulled her up from the caned stool and began to do a kind of jig in front of her. "This how you do it, Ma'am. I show you." Marion could smell the sweat coming off of Mrs. Lacey, an odor she'd been taught was offensive and dirty, an aroma that haloed only hobos and loathsome bums. But now Marion inhaled it. Her nostrils, fairly twitched to this complex of pheromones and unidentified chemicals that illuminated the woman's face as if she'd been baptized with liquid joy.

With each new breath, Marion would now file the acrid smell under Kindness, Hard Work, Love of Family, Devotion. And she took Mrs. Lacey's hands and together, they twirled around the glowing room, their faces both orange-tinted as they swooped near the fireplace, then both a deep brown as they passed into shadows. From afar, one couldn't have told one from the other.

When Marion left the little house, she thought hours had passed. The children had finally curled up on narrow bunks around the room's perimeter, or in a tiny side space where there might have been a bed. The old woman was wrapped in a shawl in her same chair, a heater in the form of a cat, placed in her lap.

"It was a wonderful evening, Mrs. Lacey," Marion told her. "Your hospitality made me feel so very, very welcomed. Thank you." The dark woman smiled softly, and closed her eyes as if taking in the words. "You can come again when e'er you like."

Lacey led the way back toward the lake, at first with the lantern, and then apparently setting it aside, by the light of the moon. Marion could hear that the sounds of the forest had changed since daylight. Now there were deep-throated voices, calls that interrupted one another, like strong men in a bar where too much testosterone might soon set off a fight. But there were other sounds she picked up: the rustlings of a restless audience among the leaves and branches, unable to keep still in their seats or on their perches, wiggling and wriggling and nibbling at pesky mites that were also aroused by the night.

Marion had been listening so intently to the *sotto voce* stirrings and the louder ones that might be alligators or owls, that she suddenly realized Lacey was not responding to her little comments on the mysteries she was finding in the woods. "Lacey? Mr. Lacey, are you up ahead?" There was no light anywhere, except the expanse of what appeared an aluminum lake, glinting back its interpretation of the moon. "Lacey! Where's the lantern?"

She stumbled across the furrowed clay and down to the lakeside bench where she'd been what felt like a lifetime ago, the place where the dark man had suddenly appeared. She had to sit down for a moment. Already, she could sense some unwanted syncopation in her heart's rhythm. She would need to get her bearings, figure out which way was out of the park, and because it appeared she had now been abandoned in the dark of night beside a reptile-infested lake, Marion would also need to decide if she should report to authorities that there was a family of Negroes squatting in a house near Lake Overstreet—that's what she'd been trained to do.

Yet these were people with whom she had just spent the happiest evening of her adult life.

Marion sat quietly on the bench for a while, blended into its wood like any one of the animals hidden among the trees. Almost as loud as the tinnitus that had begun again, were the imagined voices of the Women's Club ladies, each offering a condolence for her "awful" experience, exasperation at the gall of "those" people taking over a house, hopes that she'd had a chance to quickly wash off their sweat. And then, almost involuntarily, Marion began to hum.

At first Marion murmured in time to the little extra notes provided by her heart's rhythm section, then she set her own pace. It wasn't like Lacey's strum-can beat, but her foot began to tap, then her knee bobbed up and down. She was singing something she seemed to have known from years before, some memorized tune she believed she knew as a child.

She let her voice rise. She let herself clap the tune in this lonely place. And from the corner of her eye, Marion thought she saw that there was a cabin's light on through the trees. And further in the woods, another one—next to two others. Craning her neck, Marion saw that from the other side of the clearing, there were additional houses, and now people coming down toward the landing. They were laughing people, singing their own songs arm in arm, some with lanterns, some with towels thrown around their shoulders. They didn't address her as they high-stepped onto the dock, but they smiled and occasionally waved, voices coming in pulses as new groups created fugues and rounds.

Marion stood up and walked closer to where the people were congregating, where, filled with shouts and squeals, they were stripping down to underwear, some wrapping cloth around their hair, young boys getting naked. And then the splashes began. One after another, the party took itself airborne and plunged into the water, laughter, like droplets sparkling in the air. This was not just Lacey and his happy family. Here there was a community of joy.

"I'm so glad you could come," said the quiet voice beside her. Marion didn't move for a moment. The voice must be inside her head, she thought, because it didn't frighten her a bit. "This night is just for you, chile, you know that?" Turning slowly, Marion, saw her. Ruby May had on her blue dress and the white apron with the row of little safety pins along one side for emergencies. Her tight-stretched hair caught the lights by the water, and her eyes were filled with a smile. Marion threw her arms around the old woman, an act as natural as if a dream were dictating her every move. "Oh... Ruby May... I have missed you. I have needed you for so long."

The dark woman threw back her head and laughed, then shaking it, pulled Marion to her and stroked her back. "You gonna be fine, Mari-bee. Gonna let go and be jus' fine." Then she took Marion's face between her two long-fingered hands, and whispered in her ear, "Now, baby, time to go play. Friends be callin' for you in the water. Don't go too deep now. An' I'll be waitin' for you up here... I'll always be here, don't you worry none. Now go...."

As Marion pulled off her stockings and then her girdle, folding them into a neat pile over which she laid her dress, she watched Ruby May waving from the bank. She saw the old woman lift both hands, urging Marion to take the plunge, telegraphing a cheer and a benediction. It was a send-off that contained in it the welcome back; the same way Ruby had believed Marion could ride a bike and return whole, or step out with a boy, and not regret it. And now, there was another assignment, another place to go... and a way to return home.

Before Marion jumped into the dark waters of Lake Overstreet, she looked back at the little houses of its community. The lights had gone out now, and as the water closed over her head, she knew the laughing voices had gone faint. But it was alright. This is where Ruby would be waiting for her, with a towel, and eternal peace, and maybe, Marion thought, Lacey would come with walnuts.

"To You As Well, Signore"

Rome's life became a postcard millennia ago.
What remains is a long traffic horn and Audrey Hepburn's ghost.

The white-robed Dominican sat staring from the open
confessional, a placid mechanical gypsy oddly placed in a side aisle
of the Roman church. His hooded brown eyes, unblinking and as
sparkling as glass, seemed to beg for a quarter to initiate the
clockworks that would bring him to speech, and for me, from his
carnival hand, a prophesy of good luck.

Suddenly, while I looked for an offering coin, he stretched his
neck sideways and sat forward in the creaking cubicle. His fat
shoulders touched its walls and I wondered if he had no legs. Packed
into the half-open confessional box, the chubby cleric was surely a
huge toy, some partially-opened Christmas gift that contained this
terrifyingly large doll.

Then he raised his hand in what I took to be a kind of a royal
wave, the kind that glacially parts the air and conveys nothing.
Instead, he pointed at me, then curled his finger back toward
himself. The pudgy doll in priest's clothes was calling me over.

He waited. As I approached, he gave an intimate jerk of his
head, and with eyes that danced like sepia sequins, said, "Welcome,
me girl. What might I do for thee?" I'm sure he said, "thee."

The old priest, if indeed he was that, assured himself I had
nothing to get off my chest, then shared that he did. He was lonely,
he said. He was old, and he was lonely. And a pretty face... well,
nothing ever helped those two conditions like a pretty face.

Born in Ireland seventy-six years before, he'd been called to
serve "all over the world," he explained. "But we're a bit like wee

pieces of soap. Use us till we're worn down, melt us into shape again, and send us out to be worn down someplace else. Ah, but this is the life I chose of me own free will...." He gave a noisy sigh.

He said he could retire now, but he actually enjoyed his two hours a day hearing sinful Catholics spill their tainted moral beans in a public place.

"But I'd be claustrophobic, lass, sitting in a *closed* confessional—a box with little holes punched through the walls—staring at only a shadow. Especially one with a bonny, lilting voice, like your own, I might add." I caught his wink. But, he said, if a believer preferred not to have what the Italians call, "*i quatro occhi*", four human eyes staring across at each other, he would reluctantly leave his open booth and hear their confession in a closed hutch—"but only if the burdened soul keeps it snappy and brief!" He laughed like an elderly leprechaun deposited in the wrong body, wishing to leap about and slap his knees, but instead finding himself stuffed inside a wooden crate.

Then he laid his old hand on mine, and *his* confession was over. His color had risen as he talked with me, but now it faded, and the fixed look of innocence found on the painted saints surrounding us settled once again upon him. I reached into my purse and pulled out a two Euro coin, laying it near his hand.

A slight noise made me glance up. His lips had begun to tremble. I heard, or perhaps sensed something else start to move. With incremental pulses, his mouth now slowly opened, closed, and opened again and out of it scrolled a narrow strip of paper, that when I pulled it free, read, "Long Life, Great Wealth, and Deep and Endless Love."

Face to face, neither of us moved. I stared into his eyes, but saw only myself reflected there. Then I folded the little paper into my purse, taking it as a blessing from an old saint whose inner works still produced goodness. And from my side of his box, I whispered, "*E anche Lei, signore, anche Lei.*" And to you to, sir... if spirit, or flesh, or gears thee be...a blessing for you too.

May I Have This Dance?

Harry blew his nose, the conventional, outside way men like him had learned from their fathers was acceptable. He wiped the residual snot on the back of his hand and glanced in the right rearview mirror at his 300-pound frame. Not the best physique for a guy in his line of work, but he was agile enough for crawling under houses and into the attics of the homes he was hired to inspect. Damned good at it, in fact. Not so good at keeping a woman happy. But then guys like him learned how compensate. A six-pack and a needy carburetor on a Saturday night brought their own companionship.

He pulled the clipboard out of the cab of the truck and read down the list of houses he would look at today. First two, then maybe a third unoccupied place out along Crosby Road, a dead-end track where they said some old sharecropper had once lived. Be better to tear a heap like that down, Harry thought. But if somebody wanted to assess how bad the roof leaked, he'd let them know for a hundred bucks—just enough to clear his bar bill. Besides, it'd be another chance to use the new toy, a prize he'd won at a builder's convention a couple of weeks before. Damnedest thing he'd ever used. Seemed like it'd be better for the cops than for home inspections, but what the hell, it made the day go by faster, and God knew, there was no reason to go on back to his own empty house.

From the bed of the Ford, Harry pulled out what looked like a portable Geiger-counter with an attached TV screen, along with a measuring tape, a screw driver, and a plastic bag to collect termite crap. It was all he needed to tell a potential owner about the past life of a building and if it had been loved or not. That's how Harry felt sometimes. Alone in an abandoned house, he thought he could almost feel the boards reporting abuse, the plumbing, neglect. And he was finding that with his newfangled tool, there was even more to learn.

The first house was a tiny clapboard. Painted blue on the outside, Harry guessed it was built in the '40s, probably around the time World War II broke out. The owners here would have been happy—for a time. He took his usual measurements, looked at the welds around the old pipes, checked the attic for rat-eaten insulation on the wiring, and then he turned on "the instrument." He wasn't sure how the thing worked, but once up and going, images began to appear on its screen. He could discern wear inside window frames, weakness in wall studs, invisible flaws that showed up with a blue-lit glow. Wear, tear, oily stains, and botched repairs were revealed as if a smirking tattletale were leading Harry from room to room. Recently, he'd noticed something else. If he twisted a half-hidden dial on the bottom of the machine in a certain way, he could see in even more detail. Now, fingerprints were evident, jelly smears turned red, footprints leading from room to room as if muddy feet tramped back and forth, all showed on the little screen in his hands.

Harry looked at his watch. Maybe spend a few more minutes here, he thought, noticing where the footprints were glowing heaviest. The "blue-ray" outline of shoes showed people circling the kitchen table, where the wife stood at the sink, arms probably deep in suds. And then he saw little footprints—baby shoes. He could tell an unstable gait, maybe where there was a fall and little toe tips got dragged in a crawl. Harry could feel this house, watch the comings and goings when its residents were young and happy, and guess at the possible sorrow when the father hadn't come home from war. He turned off his instrument and drove away, wondering how many phantom footfalls had awakened a young widow, ones that hadn't left a mark.

The second house was even older, Harry'd been told, occupied by a cantankerous spinster who'd refused to leave her Victorian refuge until carried out. Harry looked forward to admiring the old building methods with the thick beams of impenetrable wood and real plaster that clung to the walls. He hoped the irascible old maid hadn't let things go. He imagined her sitting in a chair filled with mold spores, angrily poking a cat, and ignoring yellow water dripping from the tap. But he learned that things were different.

With his little dial turned to High, he began to see footprints that moved this way and that, patterns of feet, that when he actually put his own foot on one, and then another, Harry found himself turning, almost swaying, moving from print to print in what was surely a dance. Looking more carefully, he saw there were larger feet facing opposite the smaller ones, and moving in synchrony. And they were everywhere—in the parlor, in the dining room, a side porch, and even in the bedroom, where the patterns were tighter, less movement of feet, as if the old woman and her lover only swayed, maybe kissed, soon made love. Harry stood staring at the floor, feeling jealous at how the tips of their toes interlaced. He wished he could have watched them dance and repeat the pattern of their steps.

He headed out toward Crosby Road, to the last house of the day. The fields were flat here, rimmed by pine forests that were prized when the turpentine moguls held sway. Along the road, set back on even narrower dirt tracks, were lines of abandoned sharecroppers' cabins, former slave quarters they'd paid with labor to buy. Harry had been inside a few—walls covered in yellowed newsprint, running water and electricity still innovations. Although the one he was to inspect was a little bigger than the others, he had no idea why anyone would want to buy it.

He got out in front of the little porch and gathered his equipment. The sky had turned dark, threatening rain, but he turned on his instrument just for the heck of it. Just because, when all was said and done, a fat, lonely country boy had little more to do than follow other people's footprints. Harry wondered if this is how it felt to be a peeping Tom, stealing glimpses of others' lives when you don't have one of your own. Then he shrugged that he only saw what they had discarded, and he didn't turn off his machine.

But before he could even step onto the porch, Harry immediately saw them. In fact, it looked like a damned zoo. He saw quail tracks in the yard. There was a snake that had wiggled under the steps. A possum had visited, a dozen squirrels, several raccoons by the size of their feet, a fox that must be the size of a dog. Harry walked to the back of the cabin, where the machine revealed two new sets of prints—something that had four paws, and another with two human feet that had walked into the woods.

He stopped for a moment, looking around at the layers of green. Shades of olive, lime and chartreuse, the underbrush a black that turned blue in the light, and the cabin's greyed wood, striated with the reds of old pine sap as the grain had sagged into elegant undulations and swags. Suddenly Harry longed to stay here, in the quiet, in the beauty of lost things turned old without anyone being aware. He thought he'd like to do it too—just like this.

He put down his gear and the new toy that whispered the paths others had tread, and softly set out into the woods, wondering at the way ahead, yet somehow sure.

And he saw her there, just as he had expected, just as he had hoped—just as her narrow, arched footprints had predicted. A tall, black woman, alone with her pet, letting the pond's light sow diamonds in her hair. She turned to him, unafraid, with eyes that might have recently wept in goodbye to her house, but now silently acknowledged him.

And Harry, held out his hand, sure of his destination, sure of where he stood, at last knowing where he would rest, and said, "Excuse me, Miss. Would you care to dance? I can teach you where to put your feet."

The Graceful Arts

Grace Anne, Gracie Lee, and Lagracia were exchanging sidelong glances. It was late afternoon at the academy, a time when shadows turned the pink marble columns a lavender that looked almost fragrant. Yet, none of them thought of this place, their de facto home, as a place of genteel repose. Instead, it was where they worked. Where, like on-call nurses, or taxi drivers who must be ready at a moment's notice, each of them, for years now, could tell she was paying the price. Years that felt like centuries, and maybe were.

Of course, none of them wanted to be caught appraising the obvious decline of the other. Each of them hoped nobody was noticing it in themselves. But, a quick glance at a shoulder's inflated contour, the way their once softly-draped tunics now strained against flesh, not to mention the indolent stares that might entrap anyone of them for an hour or two—even as incoming calls for inspirational assistance went unanswered—all told the story of three women gone stale. Three women who were "mused" about by half the population, but who now only wanted to take a nap.

At first, it was Gracie Lee, with her Bettie Boop eyes, who opened them wide and said, "Well, Ah don't know 'bout y'all, but Ah am gist plum outta ideas. Ah ain't got nothin' new to contribute to none of 'um!" She shoved at the bun atop her head—actually more sausage than bun—which had slipped to the side and was undoing itself with each head wag. "An that's all they do, you know... Gist lay there in their beds, or go on these long country walks, or drink a bottle of gin, and expect some tale to be all tied up and ready in their noggins when they come back to their senses. "I wanna be Hemingway!" "Dostoevsky for me!" Like maybe they

135

could do some of the goldarn work themselves!" she grumbled. "I guess nobody ever heard the words, "plot outline" before?" Gracie Lee gave a jerk to the tunic that had slipped down one very large arm and scratched at her bare foot with the sole of a worn sandal. She tried to fold her arms and gaze out a window, but irritated as she was, even that was too much effort.

Grace Anne stared at her colleague and lifted her chin... chins... higher than usual. Even now, with the cadence of cow bells in the distance, bird songs among the pillars, soft breezes undulating melodies through the trees, Grace Anne could only agree with the common-spoken Gracie Lee. She, Grace Anne, professionally trained, schooled in sound by Mother Nature herself, gifted with an aristocratic sense that brought audiences to their feet to praise those whom Grace Anne had tutored, now avoided the lyre that was propped, golden and dusty against a wall. She kicked the tympanum beneath the divan when she could, and refrained from even tapping her swollen feet in any rhythm at all, because, in fact, she didn't hear them anymore.... symphonic rhythms, quartets, arias. All were muted or gone. Patterns and sequences were for her now only white noise. "Uninspired," she thought. "I can't even bob my head to a cricket's beat."

Lagracia rolled her eyes and gave her neck that special little "Z"-zag that meant, "Somebody here is waaaay under my skin." She scratched at her torqued hair, wig-hard, but durable, with fingernails she found time to polish like silver every other day. "So what if I like pretty nails," she'd retorted when Grace Anne had looked disapprovingly at the two-inch talons. "I got my body to make people love me, and I gotta take care of all its parts." In the long-ago past, when piqued, Lagracia would get up and shimmy, or grand jete, or do a couple of pirouettes just to show the difference between her graceful body and those of the other two. Although the three often collaborated with clients, it had been up to Lagracia to translate inspiration into muscle and flesh. Now, even she was filled with a torpor that had invaded and filled out her warm brown skin.

She was glad Grace Anne had abandoned music, because she had no steps to weave within the notes.

The three Graces slumped on the front porch of the temple. One flicked through her cell phone, another had begun to snore in the hammock she'd strung between a couple of fluted columns, and the third, Gracie Lee, was chewing at stumps of her nails that if Lagracia had seen it, would have made her blanch.

"There just ain't nothin' new anymore," said Gracie Lee, appearing to have homed-in on an actual thought, one she declared as if a stone-scribe should take down the words. "I mean, we done created rock-bangin' and we got them "statues" plumb all over the place now. We showed 'em how to smash berries and stuff to get color that'd stick on cloth and paper. We even made it how they know what to keep in and what to throw out to make a picture pretty. But new? Why, they're all just doin' the same danged things they've been doin' for well…eons, I reckon."

"You got that right, Baby!" Lagracia looked up from her phone, then shoved it into her cleavage. "Why, in the beginning, them old cavemen just pranced in circles around a fire, sometimes crawlin' on their bellies, rollin' and jumpin' like a bunch a crazy puppies. And now what they doin'? That same thing!" Her hands were on her hips and her neck in action. "I went to all the trouble to give 'em ideas on how to waltz and polka, and get up on their little pointy toes and twirl around, and give 'em the thought of "what if we stick metal on our shoes and make a whole lotta noise?" Ha ha, they all loved them tap dancin' folks. But now… here we are back again. Rollin' on the ground, hoppin' like rabbits in their bare feet… Oh, and they call it art, folks. Well, that's why I bailed. I can't be no Muse, if I'm not A-Mused" Lagracia slapped her ample thigh and gave an elbow to Grace Anne, who was actually agreeing with her.

"You two are exactly right," Grace Anne said in her academic accent, the one she inspired politicians to use when they spoke at the Forum… or in recent times, at White House affairs, or on Fox. "How are we supposed to inspire people if all they want to do is repeat the same two notes, retell the same story, and throw pigment at paper till the freaking cows come home?" Gracie Lee and Lagracia snapped around to look at her with concern. If Grace Anne had lost her decorum—or maybe her mind—they were all doomed.

"Well, what can we do about it?" said Gracie Lee, looking from one Grace to another. Lagracia scratched at her head again. There was silence for a moment, while the women readjusted their bra straps and seemed to gear up for action.

"I'm for somethin' radical," said Lagracia, looking up. "Somethin' that'll shake 'em down to their stiff little fingers and toes." Each of the women knitted their brows now. For the first time in years, they felt inspired by something. Felt the rebelliousness that always accompanied the onset of inspiration.

"Oh yeah…" muttered the elegant Grace Anne, hefting herself to her feet and smoothing her gown. Her lips had begun to tremble in a very plebian way, and beads of un-aristocratic sweat circled her lips. "Let's do a "mash-up!"

Querulous stares made her explain. "Why not a playwright who wants to break dance?" Grace Anne said. "Why not a bassoon player who can't stop singing? The ballerina who recites poetry? A pilot who must play the flute? Yes, yes, I have it! We can cross-pollinate them! Create hybrids! We'll make the opera star sing hip-hop. Have a fireman write a play. An aborigine star at the Met!! Oh, wait, that one's already been done…" They all nodded that Te Kanawa had worked out very well.

Grace Anne took a breath and sat down, dabbing daintily at her glowing cheeks. "What do you think, girls? I feel… I feel… how do you say it, Lagracia? "Pumped?" "Stoked?"

"Yeah, Baby!" hooted Lagracia. "And I know just what I'm gonna start with. See that boy there with his boombox on top of his backwards hat and his bad behind showing out from those saggin' pants?" She pointed to the luminous thought bubble that had appeared above her head. "This here boy is gonna need himself a dose of Beethoven!" And suddenly the young man stopped, appeared to listen to something, then put down his music box and fumbled with its dial. In seconds, the roar of the Fifth Symphony was making Lagracia's overhead bubble quiver. The boy stood up, his hands beginning to rise and fall to the music. He was conducting. He was weeping, radiant, and he seemed—delivered. "Damn! I be good!" Lagracia puffed, turning in a little circle.

"Well, you took my thunder, didn't you, missy!" Grace Anne said it with a hug to the Muse beside her who'd just tried out a little music instead of her usual dance steps. "I like that. Sure, we can do it too. We can all "mash-up." So, I'll choose. Let's see..." Above her head, a dozen images tracked across her bubble. "Oh look! There's the Vice President in the middle of a speech to the United Nations! Perfect! I'll give *him* a little blast of inspiration... Let's dance!" she squealed. And within the bubble, the three women saw the Vice President abruptly look up as if he'd heard something. Then his shoulders begin to move right, then left, and from behind the podium, he suddenly turned, kicked his right leg toward his nose, and did a front flip onto the floor of the General Assembly. Now he was spinning and leaping, Fred Astaire come to life. First a boogie-woogie beat, then, grabbing the Representative from Poland, a dramatic tango that ended only after he'd arched her backwards over Pakistan's desk, with one of her stiletto-tipped feet pointing to the ceiling, and his ecstatic face buried deep within her hair. "Oh, you done good, sweetie!" said Gracie Lee, high-fiving Grace Anne. "Now it's my turn!"

Gracie Lee had had time to think about where to shoot her inspiration while the other recipients had been conducting and dancing. And now she knew just where she'd find who would be inspired by her. Her bubble began to glow as the other Muses sat down to watch as if they'd entered a theatre.

Over Gracie Lee's head, a classroom appeared. Two dozen 12-year-olds were headed out to the playground in twos and threes. Little cliques of like-colored children, other groups with Asian eyes, or Spanish words, and several children all alone and trailing. And with a wink at the other Graces, Gracie Lee gave a little nod at the bubble. Suddenly, the formerly segregated groups were in motion. As if pods of molecules had broken free, the children ran randomly from one to the other, laughing and taking no notice of color or race. One child began to sing in Chinese. And in moments, the same song was joined, but this time in Farsi. A little Spanish child stood up and led them all until, switching languages, the Congolese girl sang the next verse. They sat down on the playground, linking arms and passing the song and its languages from child to child, somehow all of them learning the words as they went. "I am so happy!" squealed one. "I love this!" called another. "This is so inspiring!" said another girl who had once been all alone. "I want to dance! I want to sing!" "I want to paint a picture of the way we are today!" came the words from the playground.

And the three chunky women, so very far away, grasped each other's hands, themselves moving in a circle, humming first a gavotte, then snatches from a honky-tonk hit, as they kicked their legs high, and spun down low, and in each of their mind's eyes, a picture was painted, a masterpiece, a living sculpture of how they'd inspired a bit of the world to dance and how they could make it sing together.

When Women Danced With Trees

The little boys stood in a semicircle, the quivering and sniffling having died down. Their parents were behind them, some clustered together, some with their hands protectively on the boys' shoulders, hoping their own trembling wouldn't reignite the hysteria the children had carried with them out of the woods. But now, the police had brought everyone back to the scene, and like a contagious virus, anxiety as to what they all stared at was threatening an outbreak.

Flashlights played back and forth through the trees, and from time to time, one policeman would shout to another. For a moment, the glade seemed positively festive, as silhouettes skittled back and forth, and the long fingers of elms and oaks playfully interlaced in the semi-dark. Then one man separated himself from the blue-jacketed officials and came toward the small band of boys.

The man who identified himself as the Chief Inspector seemed to have a sympathetic heart as he knelt down before two little boys whose ability to articulate what they'd found hadn't been overwhelmed by the whimpering of the others. He was greyed and rumply, and Miranda guessed any child would feel safe perched on his lap. "Just tell me now, lads, what you were doing in the woods and what you first saw."

The ten-year-olds glanced at each other, perhaps wondering if a truthful explanation would land them in trouble. But after a pause, Miranda bent over her son and whispered, "Just tell the truth, Bobby.... You have been a very brave boy so far.... Go on now." And with a breath and a plunge of his cold hands deeper into his

141

pockets, the child fixed the inspector with a solid stare and said, "We saw a spirit."

**

The courtroom was freezing cold that day, she remembered. The attorney's table where she sat was sticky with the hand-grease of dozens of other defendants, or plaintiffs, or guilty or innocent parties who had found themselves lifted from their everyday lives and suspended for a time— often a long time—in this vortex of jurisprudent hell. It was the place she'd come to find justice, or punishment, though none of it would ever suit the crime.

Yet she had expected the words the judge spoke, hadn't she? She'd known all along what the outcome would be. Of the fact that the thin man was guilty, there was no doubt. But his sentence, though the judge too was horrified at the murder and rape of the child, she knew would be mitigated by one thing or another. The drugs, the mental condition, the valorous war record. It didn't matter to Aline now. Her daughter was dead. Passed away, they'd said in the paper. "Succumbed," was used. "Murder" was there too. But for Aline, the delicate girl with the crown of golden curls had— vanished. That was a better word. A tiny and brilliant spark gone out without ever dancing in the grass with flowers in her hair. Without turning somersaults in the snow or swimming in the lake. Without a butterfly taking a sip from her sweet, sweet palm and resting a while in thanks. Her daughter had vanished that day, into the woods on a sultry afternoon, and she had never returned. Vanished. Though for Aline, it didn't mean she wasn't there.

**

The Inspector glanced up at Miranda, seeming to empathize with a woman who probably had to deal with a son given to fantasies or worse. Then he patted the boy's shoulder. "Well, son, we can't see spirits, can we, but maybe you saw something else. Why were you boys so deep into these woods, anyway?"

142

Miranda wanted to know that too. Of course, without the proper supervision, only God knew what little boys would get into. She'd seen it in her two older sons, the ones at the reformatory now— probably on their way to one day joining their father at the penitentiary in Wales.

"We was doing nothing bad," said Bobby, sounding hurt and defensive. "Mum was working, nobody around, got the TV cut off.... The woods is someplace you can go to wait for something to happen. Always does. Some critter or other come along. Some sound to investigate. Like you, sir... things to find out...."

The Inspector stood up, stretched his legs, and looked toward the great tree—which appeared as wide around its girth as three men with outstretched arms. He could see the vertical ruts of the bark, so deep it seemed they would sliver the oak into a thousand narrow shards. Yet, this tree, supporting thousands of pounds of woody branches, a mighty cupola whose dome soared high into the forest canopy, was going nowhere. This tree somehow was an offeror of solace, harboring the principalities of ants, and birds, and rodents, and mites that dwelt within its protection. And it knew how to guard its own. Of that, everyone standing in the dark of the glade could surely see.

**

Aline sensed the rails' shudder beneath the train, as if the nails were coming loose, worn thin by years of supporting the comings and goings of people tearing back and forth for reasons that in a hundred years would appear pointless. It was on the train, coming back from another of the stilted visits to a father who neither recognized her, nor his food, nor his own face, nor the use of the urinal that sat dry at the end of his bed, that she opened the letter whose contents she'd been dreading since the new company bought her old one.

It was to the point. Her department was being eliminated in the interests of cost cutting. Thank you for your service, and a few well wishes sent your way. Sorry about the inability to pay severance.

More well wishes for your future employment. Oh, and fuck you, while we have your attention.

Aline sat rigidly, rocked forward and back by the wobbly cars, that, like naughty children in a file, were each trying to go off in their own direction. From the front of the train, an oily stench wafted back into the cars, or perhaps it was from the coal smelters and the decaying towns that seemed to pass like smudged aquarelles outside the window. Only the landscape gave relief. How odd she thought that the detritus of human life and fortune could lie so near the passive tranquility of these hills, undulations filled with greenery that renewed itself even as it died. She wondered if that were happening to her daughter—somewhere—reuniting, and reemerging whole. She longed to breathe in the air that was exhaled by the forest. Would it be cool, or warm—like the little clouds her child had breathed as she slept.

A tiny racket had begun somewhere under the threadbare seat of the car, and as Aline reached down to adjust a rusty heater cover that had shaken loose, she noticed another envelope that had fallen from the pile she'd shoved into her purse on the way to visit Dad. She hadn't seen this one, and its heft seemed ominous. As was its return address: *Fifth Judicial Court. Bankruptcy and Family Law Division.*

She looked out at the trees as she slowly opened the envelope, admiring their undulating branches that like fresh air anemones moved in a waterless world. She wondered at their tranquility, registering blue and green, silver leaf-bellies upturned in delight at the sun. She wondered why she was even opening the envelope in her hand—why go through the motions of shock or surprise, the anger and despair? Why pretend? When what she really wished to do was to step off of this train and walk into the woods and listen to the whispers she thought she could almost hear. And yet she read the letter

Yes, he would get the house. No, since the child was deceased, he would pay no back support. All monies in his name would remain his, even if they had once been her inheritance from the charming old uncle she had cared for long ago.

She raised her eyes to the trees once more.

**

The Inspector asked if he could take Bobby to the tiny circle of chairs where other little boys were being interviewed. It was in plain sight, and there was a matron and a doctor present, he said. It would only be for a short while. Miranda nodded and assured Bobby she would be nearby.

Yet she wanted to see for herself. The lights still moved in the darkness beyond the great tree, but for now, this largest of all the others—the one with the woman—was left unattended, bathed in a kind of violet light that as its branches bowed in the light breeze, seemed to begin a rhythm, some kind of song with a melody just out of earshot.

Miranda had never seen anything like this. Who would have? Who could have imagined such a thing? She stepped forward, and then back, trying to picture the woman as she would have approached the tree. Her arms must have been wide, in an embrace really, grasping the tree like a lover, and her cheek, even now turned to bone, laid gently against the darkened wood. Her hair was red, unloosened, and like the white gown, moved in unison with the branches overhead. She was a woman in love, perhaps, or a child needing protection, even a mother gathering strength. But as Miranda walked nearer, it was what lay around the waist and legs, across the skeletal back, what embraced the delicate head, that both frightened and thrilled her. The tree had reciprocated. The tree had understood and loved back.

Growing from the base of the trunk, new tendrils had turned to thickened branches. They wound across the woman's body, growing tighter as they reached across her torso, holding her close, binding her to it, just as she had continued to force her fingers into the bark, and the bark in turn, consumed them. A consummation, indeed, thought Miranda, an absorption of soul into soul. And she found herself at once aroused and filled with a comfort unlike any she had dreamt of. Father-protector, lover-devourer—never to be abandoned. Miranda could hardly breathe as she stared at the tree and the woman, finding herself filled with a kind of ecstasy that had begun to flow slowly—like sap.

"Over here, another one!" She had heard the shouts before, but couldn't make them out. Now, shaking herself, Miranda pulled back from the tree into the shadowed perimeter to listen to what the policemen were calling.

"There's another one over here, that makes what… twelve, so far. Jesus…. What have these women done!"

**

There is peace here. There is nothing here. There is everything here. There is emptiness here. There is peace.

Aline had been the first. The first to feel the rough bark, like a virile man, his skin toughened, his beard gone long, his power clear even as he stands—waiting. She had felt the scrape against her own skin, gasped as she laid herself against its crevices and contours and smelled the earth through which this verdant organ had erupted. And as the years moved forward, as the shoots wrapped her ankles, wound about her legs and her hips, there had been transcendence in her own decay, her gift to the tree, to the soil from which it ate, to the creatures who shared with her this bower of protection that gave her nothing—but peace.

The others had followed. Without knowing how to come to this place, without knowing what it was they sought, they had found the glade, sensing the trees that called to them, with offers that could not be refused.

**

And so it was that Miranda, one night not so long ago, came there too. Her Bobby, the best of the lot, the year before had been tossed off a bridge for stealing from the wrong man. A notice went up in the papers to be on the watch. And the hoodlums had laughed,

146

and done more stealing themselves, and done cartwheels on the spot where they'd sent Bobby flying.

She'd worn her best dress. The pretty, long one with the flowing skirt and the ivory belt. And her hair was clean as she undid the bun and shook it out to the air. She hadn't walked around the glade; she hadn't needed to. She could feel that others were near, like in a big house where the roomers are all tucked in, and you can sense them inhaling and exhaling together—a hive perhaps, except here, each with their own cell—their own tree. Their own place of permanent respite.

Miranda touched the tree. She smelled its fragrance of humus and perhaps the tiny new mushrooms that were beginning somewhere high. Closing her eyes, she tasted the bark's tannin with her tongue— a new lover's lips first explored, waited for too long, and breathed in the forest's exhalations. Softly, she whispered a prayer for the Bobby she had lost, and for the Bobbys lost everywhere. And in the quiet that filled her like the filtered light of the forest, Miranda stretched her arms around the tree, asking for its cloister—to become ant or bird or transparent spore. Waiting now for the tree to croon and to cradle her—here, where she will start again—a new shoot bound for sunlight.

GETTING AWAY FROM IT ALL

Accursed Bones

It had all started with the red wine, the thrill of babbling in French, and the mention of whale bones. A benign combination it would seem, but one that on an April evening off the Caribbean isle of Bequia, where whaling is still practiced as it has been for centuries, we and our French friends, naively or stupidly, began our stumble into sin. It was the Bones, of course. The Curse of the Bones. And we were literally about to jump in with both feet.

But first, a little history: The island of Bequia is one of several jewels in the necklace of the Grenadine chain, not far north of Trinidad. Slightly more arid than St. Vincent or St. Lucia, Bequia's outline undulates with scores of beaches where palms arch into the water, sunsets erupt like poems, and iridescent harlequin fish stare at you with heavily "mascaraed" eyes.

If one takes the bus from Admiralty Bay up the side of the mountain and around and down to Friendship Bay, the tiny fishing settlement of La Pompe tenaciously clings to the hill. Here is the one-room whaling museum run by Harold and his son, harpooner, Bentley Corea. Inside are the harpoons, the killing gun, and the icon-like photos of Bequia's famous whalers. And there are also bones. Scapulas, jaw bones, ribs, vertebrae—all remnants of the two whales per year that Bequians are permitted to harpoon as stated in agreements reached with Green lobbyists, the government of the Grenadines, and international whaling consortiums.

During the three months of February, March, and April, hump back whales migrate from New England into the warm waters between St. Vincent and Bequia. Mother whales are accompanied

151

by last year's calves, now over 26 feet long, and therefore, per the whaling agreements, fair game.

Here whales play, mate, and bask in the sun. Each year, in these waters, two will be killed, a mother and her calf. A mile away from Bequia, on uninhabited Petit Nevis, the carcasses will be winched onto land and butchered, their meat distributed to the delighted Bequians, and the whale's bones left scattered in the shallow waters beneath the rendering house.

**

After visiting the museum, several of us had dinghied over to Petit Nevis to have a look at the site—now just a ramp, a rusting winch, and a crumbling stone shed. The beach was steep and white and surrounded by tall palms. There, lying blanching in the sun, only yards from the water, was the massive baleen-draped jawbone of a whale. It was as large as a van; the meat long since consumed. But as we circled our dinghies just off the beach, we looked closer. From beneath the clear, aqua water we saw shimmering outlines. At first indistinguishable, we turned off our engines and waited. Slowly, as the water stilled, we saw them—tumbled skeletal pinwheels, hundreds it seemed. Vertebrae—tossed one upon the other, stacked like jagged poker chips. All waiting for us.

We had seen these circles of backbone in Bequian beachside restaurants. Sipping pina coladas, customers sat perched on whale vertebrae chairs; others propped their elbows on whale rib bars; most of us had walked under whale jaw arches-of-welcome. They were huge, white, primitive, and beautiful. And there was something about the local acceptance of these sculpted bones as pieces of everyday life that seemed to have anesthetized us as well. Though I hate to admit it, we wanted a vertebra of our own.

Later, as we poured from a third bottle of Cabernet, we'd discussed with our French buddies the museum, and the rendering shed, and the daunting magnitude of these wonderful beasts. The elemental beauty of living closely to the land and the sea drifted over us all. We all ate fish freshly caught, pulled mangos from trees, boiled up wonderful roots we'd never eat at home, and filled our boats with flowers we hacked fresh from jungle glades. In this setting, the plan of taking home a symbol of the grandeur of the ocean—a vertebra—didn't seem so far-fetched. It was as if we'd all come under a sort of spell in which we no longer countenanced the arguments Green Peace might have shouted in our ears. Though we had declined a bracelet of tortoise shell that very day, and had never even carried home a sand dollar, all of us somehow were transfixed with the whale bones. And we decided to go fetch ourselves one early the next day.

**

The sky was clear as we set out in two dinghies. For cruisers, whose idyllic, but sometimes monotonous days find a thrill in a friend's new water pump, the adventure of diving for "organic" treasure had us at a high pitch of excitement. With one dinghy powered by a 25- horsepower engine, the other, a soft-bottomed skiff with a tiny four-horsepower engine, we gathered snorkel gear and rope and leapt in—wide-eyed and filled with wonder at nature's beneficence.

What we didn't know was that the "Whale gods" were now on alert and readying a series of pointed signs guaranteed to teach us all a lesson.

Though only a mile to Petit Nevis, the passage is open to the ocean from the east. Today the seas were high, running up to six feet. The larger engine, riding the waves, slid its dinghy and the two occupants across the swells, and ultimately into the lee of the island. But the Frenchman's smaller dinghy, so underpowered for the conditions, seemed to have suddenly vanished even as we watched. Before our eyes, the little boat had apparently capsized. Turning our dinghy around, we fought back through the breaking waves, and at the moments we mounted the crests, began to see him clinging to his little white raft. He must have gone "airborne" as the baby engine's propeller was lifted out of the water. The Frenchman had simply sailed out the side and into the water, thankfully pulling out

153

the ignition key with his wrist strap as he went. We hauled him in and cautiously towed the little dinghy into Petit Nevis' calm.

If we'd correctly read this first signal the Whale Gods had given us, we'd have had a bite of cheese and crackers at this point and turned around and gone home. But we still were individually harboring visions of whale bone coffee tables, whale vertebra breakfast stools, or maybe a large and wall-buckling whale bone clock. We therefore proceeded in our hunt with the zeal of a trio of bumbling Mel Fishers.

The men, working together in snorkel gear and gloves, brought up three 50-pound vertebrae. Slung over the sides into the dinghies, the bones were still covered with tissue, and reeked with the leathery smell of rotting flesh. Fish were everywhere, including two blacktip sharks who skeptically watched the operation.

Stretching three-feet across and two-feet wide, each vertebra had a flat circular center that was porous and, we decided, perfect for a striped cushion. Thoughts of how these animals had suffered, strangely, were very much on our minds. Even as we mentally decorated our living rooms, we stared into the water with a deep sadness that such magnificent creatures had died to create a few Bequian harpoon-heroes for a day. Oddly, we exempted ourselves from judgment as we continued to sort out our haul, discarding the bones we considered imperfect, and gazing like Midases at our glistening, stinking treasures.

But the Whale Gods had now taken a deep interest in our pillage, and they had plans. As we started to haul our trusty Danforth anchor from the lava-bed below, a sudden swell hit us, and with the extra tension on the line, must have dug the anchor into the rock like a hammered piton. Both men dove and pulled. We attached another line to the bow of the Frenchman's boat and tried to back the anchor out—but the little Danforth simply declined to budge. After twenty minutes, the Frenchman, giving up with a Gallic shrug, blew through his lips and murmured, "*C'est la vie….*" Anyway, the odor from the bones was beginning to attract flies, and the magnitude of cleaning our prizes was dawning on us. With this realization, we too said goodbye to a really nice little anchor and headed for our boats to pick up scrapers and brushes and lots and lots of bleach. We were still behaving like innocents with a science project.

**

After a quick *salade nicoise* and a discussion as to how long it would take to scrape Mother Nature off of our soon-to-be coffee tables, the American contingent set off for a section of beach where we could land the vertebrae and make them ready for company. Our French companion decided to hang his loot from the propeller of his boat and do a submerged cleaning. But since a capsizing and a lost anchor hadn't been hints enough, the Whale Gods now got ready for a little more action.

In the volcanic Grenadines, the beaches drop off sharply— sometimes as much as 100 feet. This causes a hefty wave pattern that can swing a dinghy sideways or work to swamp it if one isn't careful. Scanning the beach for a forgiving place to land, we rose and plunged, motoring back and forth, ominously drifting ever closer to shore even as we were being swept broadsides to the waves. Suddenly, out of the trees darted a tiny man dancing down the beach and waving us in.

As we rose up and down on the swells, the little gnome, whom we came to know as Bernard, was running toward us in the surf. With arms flapping and an incongruous, pink blouse ruffling behind him, he stuttered and yelped that we should bring the dinghy in "Right here! Right here! Best place!" Bernard, we later learned, was a goatherd and village oddity who knew nothing about the sea or the surf. On reflection, he may have been the agent the Whale Gods were using to vent their wrath, but we did as he said and pointed the dinghy where he directed.

With a four-foot surge now breaking over the stern of our inflatable, we feared its flip and the loss of our prizes—not to mention ourselves. Bernard was spinning in circles on the beach and now pointing to another spot he liked better. Then as the dinghy plunged and spun, water pouring over the sides, the bones and I were somehow floated over the pontoon and into the warm, salty waves. With the "superhuman" strength of an Australian lifeguard, I managed to get my elbow under the tied-together vertebrae and swim them to shore.

Running back through the water to help pull the water-filled dinghy up onto the beach, I now found it totally out of control, with my friend being battered like its sparring partner. Lightened of its weight, it was an angry colt, kicking and flinging itself in every direction. One of its bucks landed the propeller hard against my leg. Even in the water I could feel the pain start. With Bernard's squealed admonitions, we finally manhandled the dinghy to shore.

By this time, amidst the screaming and grunting, Bernard's tiny herd of goats had galloped away. And as I glanced down the beach at a disappearing tail, I also noticed our baling bucket, an oar, and one of my shoes happily escaping as well.

At least I'd retrieved my scraper and bleach. I'd tied a scarf around my bleeding leg, and figured that the ominous softness in the dinghy was just a nick that wouldn't let the whole thing collapse for a while.

Now, all that remained were several hours of blister-provoking scraping, and I bent over to dig out my supplies. That's when the Whale Gods winked one more time. As we three stared down at the stinking vertebra ready for its surgery, one of my most cherished gifts suddenly dropped into the sand. A gift from my father, a beautiful pearl earring, dropped from my ear and promptly disappeared. No matter how we dug and excavated, the pearl was simply gone. Finally, I sat down and cried.

Bernard had now tied his pink blouse around his head, Carmen Miranda-style, and was jumping from one foot to the other, while my friend stood looking quietly distraught. I simply couldn't stop sniffling beside the two immense, white pieces of spine that looked so out of place on the beach. My friend patted Bernard on the back and said he'd help him look for his herd. And I decided to have a little talk with the Bones.

I'd realized, I said, that I didn't really want the vertebrae after all. That it was clear they needed to stay on Bequia. That I understood they didn't want to go. Through my tears, I had the feeling the bones were listening. (Yes, the whole adventure had brought me to this point). I told them that I released them. I told the two stinking backbones I was sorry I'd taken them from their final resting place, that they should remain in Bequia, and I hoped they would forgive me and now please remove their Curse. Hoping for the benevolence of the bones, I stood up, blew my nose, and hobbled into the brush to help locate goats.

**

But the Whale Gods had one final surprise. As we came out of the scrubby woods, leading goats and carrying scraping supplies back toward the dinghy, there stood a tough-looking local, arms crossed aggressively, marijuana cigarette dangling from his lips, and gold jewelry glinting in the sun. "So what are those scraping supplies for?" he demanded. Without waiting, he answered his own question. "I know it's for the bones. I saw where you put them. Do you know you're in big trouble? You're thieves, aren't you?!"

I told him honestly, that yes, we'd picked up the bones, but hadn't been aware there was some prohibition. Not only that, we didn't want them anyway. They were cursed!

At that, the thug's eyes widened, and he couldn't suppress a grin. I almost read his mind—"This is gonna be easier than I thought." But he kept up the pressure. "The bones have to go back!" he proclaimed, eyeing two companions who had now caught up. "You can't just leave them here on the beach. You give me $40, and I'll take them back," he said. I looked at the other two.

"That's ridiculous," I said. "I can take them back myself."

He pulled himself up with the authority of the practiced extortionist, staring me straight in the eye. "Who trust you, mon?"

157

he demanded. And then, he said something that during the whole day long I hadn't thought about.

"Those bones belong to the whalers who go out and risk their lives to catch whales," he said. "We use every piece, mon. We eat the meat, we drink the oil, why shouldn't we sell the bones when they get dry? Who you, that you be comin' in here and takin' somethin' you didn't work for?"

And he was so right.

My friend and I went back to the main vessel and returned with a tip for Bernard and some "bone-money" for the enterprising beach warden and his posse who waited with a power boat in case we hadn't produced. It didn't seem worth mentioning that he was not only getting $40 for possibly doing nothing, but in fact, that we'd made him—certainly not a whaler himself—a gift of some obviously valuable bones. But all of that didn't matter.

What was important was that at last we'd understood something so basic that in our selfish obliviousness, we'd missed the message of the bones. If anything could lessen the suffering of the beautiful animals that were sacrificed to harpoons and knives, it is that the suffering of others, their poverty and despair is lessened for a time. As if of one heart, the Bequians merge as a country at the time that a whale is killed. They are proud of their brother harpooner's skill, of his brave heart, and of the way he has provided for them all. We as foreigners have no part in that. To us, the bones were to become clever artifacts in our clever lives. For the Bequians, the bones are dynamic. They provide and they are respected.

Soon, we sailed away from Bequia. I don't know if the Frenchman kept his haul or put it back. We told him to do the right thing. In our case, a whole month has gone by and no one has drowned, nothing has been lost, and the engine hasn't seized.

I think it's very likely that our little crook put the bones back, and that at last, the Whale Gods can take a day off.

This story was originally published in the St. Petersburg Times

Aegina and the Man in a Box

The Saronic Islands are a chain of rocky outcrops stretching into the Argosaronic Sea, less than 17 miles southwest of Piraeus, Athens' premier passenger port. Curling like a cupped hand around the curve of the Peloponnesian peninsula, this scattering of mountainous islands, Hydra, Poros, Spetses, and Aegina, is each worthy of a starring role in a glossy Greek guidebook.

While the glitzy islands of Mykonos and Santorini reel in the highrollers and night-life-loving crowds, it is on islands like easy-to-get-to Aegina that one can a find a dozen storybook villages, exquisite beaches, and one of the most magnificent temples in the ancient world.

Only six by eight miles, little Aegina today greets its visitors with a circle-shaped harbor dotted with azure tables and umbrellas that dance in the wind. Sailboats line the quay, bobbing beside green and orange fishing boats whose owners each day haul in squid, octopus, and slithery eels. Maria, a husky-voiced vegetable seller, spreads racks of fruits and legumes from her houseboat onto the sidewalk and winks as she adds extra figs or pears into a buyer's sack. Her little boy, with skin the color of butterscotch, meanwhile stuffs a ripe apple into his shirt.

Aegina Town, and to the south, the more resort-like Agia Marina, bustle with people eager to pull you into their daily lives, happy to tease, and willing to laugh at themselves. But there is a deep religiosity here as well. In Aegina, during the early 1920s, the last proclaimed saint of the Orthodox Church, Saint Nectarios, lived and worked. One of the largest monasteries in the Balkan world sprawls in his honor overlooking the ancient village of Paliachora, and every Sunday a mostly black-garbed file of the faithful winds its way there to pray.

But the ancient world worshipped as well, and on Aegina it left a legacy that in structural grandeur rivals the Acropolis itself. The mighty Temple of Aphaia sits on a hill surrounded by wind-sculpted pines, the complex soaring upward in dazzling white limestone, preserved like a stony creamsicle that will never melt.

While female statues from local archeological digs recline in the Aphaia Museum, the famous "archaic smiles" softening their features, the heroic warriors of the period stand staunch, seeming to remember a time when this tiny island was Greece's first capital. Current residents take life easier, basking in the sun or slumbering in the shade of a pistachio tree.

On a cool street splashed with lavender shadows and bougainvillea buds, lifelong nut merchant, Kostos Ganas only knows pistachios. Sitting in front of his store, the weathered sienna of his face and the cerulean of his little wooden chair make him look like a painting. From his little throne, he extols the varieties of Aegina's most famous export. "Honeyed pistachios, salted ones, glazed. Pistachios in custard, jellies, ice cream… or covered with sesame seeds and kept in your pocket all day long! Pistachios will bring you health and long life and make you want to return!"

Just then, a woman dressed in black with curly white hair arrives. Kostos introduces her as his Aunt Sofia, one of the older generation who strive to keep tradition alive. She has just come from a coaching session with young village girls who are learning about the "burning of Leidinos," a coffin-encased effigy that will be incinerated as a kind of goodbye to the easy living of summer—and a caution as to the scarcity that winter will bring.

Sofia's black dress seems misleading. Inside it, there is the impression of a still vibrant woman whom one can imagine dancing with Anthony Quinn on a windy beach and shouting "Oopah" to a throbbing bouzouki. There is something about the way Sofia shoves fugitive strands of white hair toward her bun, then tosses her head to set them free again. Something about the way she glances out toward the boats, aligned like long yellow, red, and blue cupcakes, and at the old men who stand in huddles discussing weather or fish.

Kostos glances at me, then winks in the direction of his aunt. "Sofia," he calls, making a little air-circle with his finger. Then he reaches down to an ancient tape deck and punches a button to begin a pulsing, fingering of a stringed instrument whose blend of melancholy and sun seems to flow up from the white beach and thread its way through the shady pistachio trees. Kostos takes a round sheepskin-covered percussive instrument from a hook and keeps time with a hand as leathery as the drum.

Kostos has asked Sofia to dance, and with a little sigh, the elderly woman leans for a moment against a table holding candied nuts. She takes a breath. She needs to be convinced. And it doesn't take much. With only a glance at the waterfront, she begins to sway, slowly snapping her fingers, moving in place before the tiny shop, placing one stockinged leg before the other in what might be a melancholy dance for Leidinos, or perhaps a dance of longing for a world she once knew, when the cold wet winter was only foreshadowed, before the lonely years of age arrived.

Sofia leaves us behind as she moves, her neck bending in time to the music, her black skirt beginning to lift as she twirls in a slow-motion undulation, emulating the sweep of the lute and the strings, and the throb of the drum. From somewhere a shopkeeper claps, and Kostos plays, and the old men, each with their hands crossed behind their backs, wander off in their separate directions, never turning toward the little pistachio store, their heads perhaps too filled with memories of torn nets and fish they never caught.

Abruptly Sofia stops, the signs of nostalgia and melancholy disappearing from her face. She laughs out loud and turns to her nephew saying, "Yes, Kostos, the old is good, we will never lose it, and hardships are nothing we do not know. But today, the autumn sun is shining, and the sea gives us only its song. So, let's have a bit of retsina, shall we? Retsina, some salted pistachios, and the blessing of a saint." Then with a glance at the receding silhouette of an old man, she says, "Yes, pistachios. On Aegina, these are far better to think of than winter, or crusty Liedinos in his box, or others who never knew where to cast their nets, or where the nuts grew sweetest."

One Earth's Turn in Tanzania

At night, the orange wind that chases daytime dust devils across Tanzania's Serengeti plain turns stronger, causing the tents to bend in and snap out, and the lions' moans to carry.

On this night, the full moon cast shadows of acacia trees among the tents. And each time the wind paused—something close by was breathing.

Enormous Cape buffalo were lowing near the cook tent 100 yards away. But the rhythmic sound that had me scanning the darkness was close, filled with a hungry moisture that rattled in its throat. It was when I slowly lifted my head just over the top of the pillow, that through the tent's light screen mesh, the huge head appeared. The panting hyena and I evaluated each other for moments. Maybe I had very long teeth, it might have thought. Maybe I could fly through the top of the tent. Maybe I was just too skinny and not worth the effort. But with a snort, and maybe a shrug, the hyena galloped away—only to be replaced within the hour by a herd of elephants munching their way through our camp with low rumbles of pleasure. It felt as if the predators, and the masticating monoliths, and I were part of the same carnival of animals, which moved back and forth in a diorama, while dozens of others waited in the wings for their turn on this ancient stage.

This was not the Africa of the North, where in Tunisia, Libya, and Egypt the issues of man trump those of nature. Nor of the South, whose Johannesburg and Cape Town are sophisticated, skyscrapered, reeling in traffic and trade. Rather, Tanzania, situated halfway down the continent's eastern coast feels like an animal-filled park—actually 13 parks and conservation areas—peppered

163

with occasional towns. Thirty percent of Tanzania has become a preserve of desert, forests, and lakes.

Yet there is a dichotomy between ancient migrations, pastoral tribesmen, and plentiful resources for a human population dwelling within its means, and the twenty-first century with its throb of progress—the ringing of its cell phone and its tweets. Witness Barak Obama's face painted lovingly on the side of a bus, and a curio stand called *The Hil-Ary Clintan Shop*, as well as the hundreds of NGOs bringing supplies and agendas of all kinds to the sides of Lake Victoria and Kilimanjaro's slopes. But Tanzania, so far, seems to have floated free of the tumult elsewhere in Africa. Instead, it retains a kind of innocence—a special connection to the natural world.

A little time spent inside a Maasai village was to feel Africa come alive inside and out. Here, as everywhere I went, people stroke you, strangers give you hugs. And as the people touch you, so does the earth. It decorates your face; it lives inside in air swirling with an aerosol of fine red dust that you breathe in and find tucked between your toes.

That intimacy with nature is how I happened to drink some blood from the neck of a cow.

While women do the work, the proud male warriors of the Maasai, tall, wrapped in red-checked cloth, never without their spear and their cattle-herding *rungu*, wander sometimes hundreds of miles from home as they move beloved cows to ever-better pasture.

But if you've just given birth, or are feeling sickly, a cow comes in handy for a dose of iron too. I had mentioned to my guide that I wasn't feeling well, and with only a little fuss, a young cow was selected from the herd and pulled into the acacia corral. A warrior at its tail and another holding its head, a tourniquet was quickly wrapped around its neck and its jugular vein engorged. Then in an ancient rite, a tiny arrow was sharpened, and using a bow from about a foot away, the vein was pierced. A tiny spigot of blood flowed into a long gourd half-filled with cow's milk. With a smile and good wishes, the warrior watched as I sipped the mix—warm, sweet, and thankfully, without clots—while the nonplussed cow casually wandered away. But the women seemed excited. With high-pitched ululations they hugged me and pressed into my hand a kind of wand with the tip of a cow's fluffy tail on its end. It was their way of bonding the guide said—a thank you for joining willingly in a timeless ritual they were eager to share.

And it is that connection—earth, animal, man—that lingers with me when I think of Tanzania. The leopards and cheetahs, the lions and elephants, hyenas—man—all living from the earth's resources, sharing them with each other, and suffering when the earth withholds.

And the future? Perhaps the traditions will not die. Hopefully the animals will remain, vegetarians and carnivores alike. But watching a beautiful Maasai youth jump into the air, ears pierced with exquisitely carved bone, his spear held high against the blue sky—and his cell phone flying loose from beneath his robes—I pause, and sigh, and I wonder.

Being Kuna

The knock on the door of the luxury Central American residence in Panama City's toney Patilla district jarred me awake. I was visiting a friend on my way to the country's San Blas Islands—a cluster of islands about as far from the insulated and upscale Patilla area as Park Avenue is to Patagonia. These sea-level islands are home to the Kuna Indians, an ethnically pure people living the traditional lives of their Carib Indian ancestors. And with only a short hop by air and permission from the presiding Kuna authorities, I would be allowed onto the island for a few days. I'd been told that someone would come to my mainland address to pick up the fee and let me choose what I would like to eat during my stay. It sounded like a trip to Disney World, and I expected an official tourist bureau agent with a smile, a menu, and the bill on the other side of the door.

Until it swung open. The visitor before me had arrived via airplane and taxi just before midnight. She had come to collect the money for the Hotel San Blas, alright, and to suggest food for my stay which would be harvested, speared, or pulverized just before I arrived. Her name was Rubiela and she was a Kuna Indian. Short, no more than four-and-a-half-feet tall, dark and squarely built, she was ablaze with color even in the porch light. I stood mesmerized.

At first, this tiny being seemed like a child dressed-up for Halloween, but one look at the solemn gaze of a born businesswoman, and I went for my purse. Surreal or not, Rubiela could cross centuries when it came to commerce.

Smiling sweetly, the tiny Kuna shifted the red and yellow scarf covering her black crop of hair. A thick gold nose ring, the size of dime, glinted in the light. While she counted my money, I appraised the rest of her clothing. Brilliantly patterned blouse with *molas* sewn on front and back, golden coins dangling at her neck, a skirt like a crazy quilt, and tiny bands of beads covering her forearms and calves. And to heighten her beauty, there were two flaming circles of rouge on her cheeks and a tiny black line running down her nose. She was spectacular. She stood there tiny and secure, waiting to know if the fishermen should spear lobster or fish for my dinner, and like a metaphor for the San Blas Kuna themselves, not really caring what the mainlander would choose to do, only happy to be going back to her islands and a culture that had for centuries defied change and intrusion.

A few days later, two sleepy friends and I boarded the 6am flight for the 50-mile hop to the San Blas Islands. We decided that the $62.00 roundtrip fare was a bargain. After all, in one hour it was flying us to not only another century, but really, to another world.

In a prop plane seemingly made of heavy paper, we dipped and soared along Panama's northern coast. The flight would make the local run across mainland villages, and once we were dropped off, go on to the guerrilla-filled province of Darien near the Columbian border. Now, only minutes after takeoff, the plane had turned and was headed out to the archipelago of the San Blas—350 islands, some no more than powdered-sugar knolls, bristling with palms, and maintained and operated by the Yala Kuna Indians themselves. This small, but proud people had successfully withstood the Panamanian government's control in 1925 and secured the right to self-govern within the Panamanian nation. But cultural isolation is a two-edged sword.

As the plane banked to land, the rising sun turned the sea a shimmering salmon, and already we could see Kuna canoes with transparent sails heading out to fish. Their fierce independence and fidelity to the ways of their ancestors have left the Kuna culturally pure, but dependence upon the land and the sea alone for survival is a struggle. Bowing to the realities of economics, the Kuna had begun to gingerly invite tourists to visit their archipelago three decades ago. Though welcoming and warm, we would never quite lose the feeling that we were strictly invited guests. We would live nearly shoulder-to-shoulder in their village for the next week, but clearly, we were expected to mind our manners and, like good houseguests, not overstay our welcome.

But welcomed we felt when we saw tiny Rubiela enthusiastically waving to us as we set down on the 500-foot airstrip scratched out of the beach scrub of the main island of El Porvenir. The wind whipped her scarves as we hoisted our luggage into a dugout that settled to within inches of the water's surface. A boy of about 12 was at the outboard, dressed in hand-me-down urban grunge. He babbled at Rubiela in Kuna, made her laugh, and then shoved our wobbling craft into the surf. The two sparred and giggled all the way to our island, and we learned this is as much "being Kuna" as wearing a nose ring. The Indians are nothing if not social. With jokes, poetry, gossiping, storytelling, teasing, chanting—as facially animated as professional comedians—the Kuna amused themselves endlessly.

Twenty minutes later, the island of Nalunega, "Red Snapper Island", appeared to swell up out of the sea. Rubiela waved at four women on the shore dressed exactly as she was. All reds and yellows and jungle green, the women literally sparkled in the sunshine. They were identical at first glance, with slight variations in pattern and style of their dress, but they were also totally different. Two of the four women were albinos, known as "Children of the Moon." Albinism has a high prevalence among Kuna, who for cultural reasons have decided not to marry outside their own group. But despite their startling difference, the freckle-faced redheaded Kuna albinos are accepted as special individuals with special powers and often respected for their knowledge and curing chants.

As we landed our luggage, we were passed by busy Kuna launching fishing boats. Darting Kuna children ran here and there with balls of thread for their mothers who sat in every doorway stitching *molas*, the multi-colored, fabric pictures of layered cutouts. We soon reached the San Blas Hotel where the thatched roof hostel and indigenous bamboo guesthouses perched at the water's edge. We choose the Kuna House, a circle of thin bamboo reeds lashed together, a palm frond roof, three hammocks and a sand floor. The sea-breeze air-conditioning that filtered through the walls didn't hurt a bit either.

It was nearly noon now and we could hear a combination of what sounded like liturgical chanting, laughter, and squeals coming from someplace inside the village. There wasn't a guide in sight. We were on our own it seemed. And after an initial period of shyly not wanting to intrude into village life, we ambled down the tiny, winding alleyways of identical round bamboo huts where the chanting grew louder and gave onto the central open space around which the village's huge reed buildings squatted. Here the laughter swelled to a roar.

Rubiela had evaporated earlier saying she had important business to attend to, and we'd pictured her in her hut somewhere quietly rubbing her hands together as she counted profits from many *molas*. Instead, we found her at party central! The village square was filled with scores of women. In this matriarchal society, most of the traditional days of celebration are associated with female rites of passage. We had arrived as the Kuna prepared for the one of the biggest. The puberty-rite celebration involves a haircutting ceremony, followed by a communal feast and 48 hours of the nonstop consumption of *chicha*, a corn syrup and coffee-based alcohol that effectively fells the entire village by party's end. For now, Rubiela was taking her turn stirring the fermenting brew in what appeared to be cast-iron witches' cauldrons, and she motioned me towards her.

While many Kuna do not speak Spanish, Rubiela was able to make me understand that she would like to introduce me to three of the girls who would soon be the center of the celebration. She led me across the square and into a large thatched home. She winked as she pointed to a rectangular, leafy enclosure inside the house, and

169

from around the corner of this *surba*, peeked three young women—all painted black. Sequestered for the eight days it takes for the *chicha* to brew, the girls are instructed by village women in the ways of Kuna womanhood. These giggling girls, despite their color—thanks to the *genipa* fruit and the magical properties of the new moon—seemed to think it was a sleepover!

But our lobster lunch had just been snatched from the ocean, and the huge dinner bell had begun to ring. With little hugs, we had to leave the girls with promises to dance at their celebration in a few days.

The idyll of a San Blas visit is all about a stereotypic Paradise. Days filled with anthropomorphic clouds grazing their way across a shockingly blue sky, coconut palms that spill down sustenance with promising thuds, and a beneficent sea offering seascapes framed by craggy rocks and sprawling sands. For tranquility, there's nothing not to like. On each of the smaller islands, a small band of Kuna greet us for our daily outings. Toting children, shredding cabbage from the mainland, repairing sails, the men and women divided the chores equally. Men traditionally fish and make clothes for male children. Women fetch fresh water, cook and sew for girls—and of course, produce *molas*. On these slow-motion outlying islands, the village counsel continues the equality by designating one family group at a time for a three-month stay on the main island, the only venue where visitors are allowed to spend the night. Thus, the tourist income is rotated. The ubiquitous *molas* have become a staple sales product as much as fish or corn to the mainland. And the dollar per person beach fees probably account for some of the broad smiles at our arrival.

We'd seen a departing Swedish family who had actually "rented" the entire island before we'd arrived. Living like Robinson Crusoes in three-sided thatched houses with their Kuna hosts supplying fresh pineapple and grilled fish, the Swedes had bid goodbye with the gauzy gaze of blissed-out wanderers who could no longer pronounce words like, "computer" or "deadline." The Kuna hosts looked like happy bankers.

But no matter how financially savvy, at every turn there was magic among the Kuna. Nights were soft and starless on the San Blas. Back on Narlunega, after our third lobster dinner in as many evenings, we strolled unaccompanied through the darkened village where only kerosene lamps lit the cathedral-height interiors of the houses. The chanting we had heard the day of our arrival had continued sporadically, and now we found ourselves beside the house from which it came.

Peeking into the shadows, we saw a *curadaro*, a shaman-specialist in healing chants, sitting beside the hammock of a sick child. He had been chanting for at least four days. He wore a bowler hat and emphasized his incantations with a tall *nuchu*—a stick with a human carving at the top. Other magic-imbued *nuchus* were piled beside the child. The worried family smiled at us wanly as we left. We learned that most Kuna medicine is made from mainland plants and western physicians are rarely sought. We hoped the sick little girl would be able to celebrate her haircutting ritual when she turned fifteen.

By the next morning we knew that the three "dyed" girls we'd seen in the *surba* would be in for an exhausting celebration. Dugouts had arrived all the previous night from other islands, and already the spirit-flute players were in their special hammocks, lined up like so many cocoons inside the "puberty house." Every villager had contributed to the great feast that precedes the distribution of the *chicha*, and had brought their own hollowed-out calabash-gourds for the drinking marathon that would follow. With a devilish smile, Rubiela had issued us what might be called "guest-calabashes," whose great volume we could never have guessed.

As the sun went down, and the feast-fed Kuna began to shuffle toward a split sail through which the three girls' blackened arms could be seen serving the *chicha*, the flutists came to life. They had abandoned their initial droning, and now the music grew wilder as the brew poured out of the caldrons. Men and women wearing feathers and pelican bones danced in circles, stomping and whirling into tight knots, while young men imitated animal leaps and lashed themselves with thorny vines. And the *chicha* flowed.

It kept on flowing until the next evening, by which time only a very few young men were capable of making it to the split sail bar. The rest of the village, old men, octogenarian women, mothers with children, flutists, chanters, and dignified headmen were sprawled in various states of dramatic intoxication throughout the village. Our lobster dinners—any dinners—had come to an abrupt stop, since the cook was now draped over a log in the village square. Even Rubiela, always in control, was collapsed in what appeared to be a laundry basket of red and yellow fabric. We counted four snoring heads in the pile, two of them albino.

It was a little later, while we were scavenging in the hotel kitchen for some peanut butter and crackers, that we heard the tiny sound. It was a sweet tinkling, a fragile laugh, light and weak, but a laugh just the same. Peering at us through the screened door was a little form held carefully by an old man. Opening the door, we found the man in the bowler hat and the little child, now apparently on the way to recovery. She eagerly munched the gooey peanut butter and stale crackers we gave her and giggled at us shyly from behind her fingertips. Her hair was matted from her days of sickness, but we were sure it would grow to be very beautiful one day when the Kuna women came to cut it—to carry on another of the traditions that have sewn this culture into a fabric every bit as complex as an intricate *mola*.

This story was originally published in the St. Petersburg Times

The Artisans of Florence

Rarely is there a time when Florence does not pulse with life. Seldom an hour when the vast square in front of the Duomo, or scores of other Medici-touched public spaces, are not teeming with tourists, musicians, beggars, dogs, and elegant, bronzed Florentines all rushing in a kaleidoscopic cat's cradle of activity.

But in some places, down cool alleys where the sun drifts in as if it were dreaming of the long nights of Northern Europe, there is another cadence. Here, tourists are few and passers-by are more likely carrying a *panina* for lunch than a Gucci bag or tiny plaster David. These are the winding streets of the artisans of Florence, where clothing, gilded picture frames, painted maps, jewelry, and a host of other hand-made specialties are crafted exactly as they were centuries ago. Time moves more slowly here.

On the southern side of the Arno, within hailing distance of the Pitti Palazzo, in the burgos of San Spirito and San Frediano, lie the *lavoratori*, the workshops of men who seem to have tumbled bodily out of the Renaissance. In scores of two and three-person storefront *botegas* men are bent over tasks requiring patience and devotion. Here artisans appear to ignore the last two or three hundred years of technology and continue to construct time-consuming masterpieces with tools da Vinci or Galileo would have had in their ateliers.

Just across the Santa Trinita Bridge, in a dark workshop which, at first glance, resembles a Neolithic cave, hang strips of fur as thick as stalactites. Bits of sable and mink, muskrat, yellow rabbit, and turquoise beaver dangle from the ceiling or are draped on chairs in graceful swags. Dyed fur is pinned to coats and glued to hems, or tossed across the shoulders of slouching, fabric mannequins.

Gionata Cozzi, his glasses thick and smudged, already has a good idea of what fashionable, (and very rich) women will be wearing in three years. For them, he is designing and making classic full-length fur coats, or he is attaching jagged applications of lynx and ocelot to stark white leather. With a wave of his arm, he says that the brilliant aquarelled furs in the corner will go to a slightly lower-end market.

Gionata works alone here—alone except for the presence of his former master, his elderly father, Aldo, who taught him the craft of working with skins. Now 80, Aldo comes every day to sit in the corner and observe his son washing ermine tails and smoothing leather onto the women's dress form, as if he were fitting it back onto the animal which had worn it in the first place.

The slightly organic smell of wet fur mixes with that of frothy cappuccino, and the effect is cozy and slightly stifling. In Italian, the elderly Aldo says that he had learned this craft from his uncle, who had been taught by his father and grandfather before him. "If you want what everyone else is wearing, pieces made by machines in an hour, you go one place. But here…." Aldo kisses his fingertips and smiles at his son, "Here, you will find the perfect fit, the perfect coat!" And you understand that for Aldo, time ticks slower, like the pealing of the campanile, measured by good conversation and the mastery of a smooth seam.

As Gionata Cozzi carefully cuts a hank of glove-soft leather, his father wonders aloud, as will the other artisans, if his craft will last another 50 years. "Machines are jealous of us," he says. He stares at a swath of spotted fur, soft and full, and fingering it, says that the 1930s was his favorite decade. "Then, every woman wanted a fur, and men knew that such a fur was the key to a woman's heart! *Un buono decennio*!"—a good 10 years. Then Aldo works his way toward the back of the shop, touching each skin as he passes, like a friend reaching out for the warmth of kindred spirits.

The Piazza San Spirito, with its important, but nondescript church façade, is the site of a daily vegetable, flower, and used-clothing market. Beneath leafy lindens, the vendors look alternately bored and animated, but always ready to adjust their prices a little, "just for you." To the right of the square, through doors thrown open to catch the spring light, sits a man called Roberto.

Roberto Beli sits at his treadle-vice, afternoon sun illuminating worn wooden tools. If an arc of gold leaf were placed behind Roberto's head, he would surely become a medieval saint; close your eyes and his long aquiline nose and halo of curls transform him into a monk or a martyr. But Roberto is neither. Instead, he blends an ancient artisan's craft with a modern milliner's needs. Roberto carves from wood the hat forms upon which layers of wet felt or straw will be draped and baked to create sophisticated headpieces for those in the world who need a $500 hat.

With his brother, Luciano, Roberto says that he turns out "about 100" hat forms each season. Receiving sketches from top-scale milliners in Paris, Rome, and London, the Beli brothers, after careful study of the designs, are able to carve out of a limewood bloc, the creases, dimples and swirls that capture in wood the exact look of a nascent high-fashion hat. Only 15-20 hats will be made from each sculpted form, and the thought of a machine-stamped chapeau make the brothers snigger in derision.

Under the red-brick gothic vaulting of this workshop, Roberto points to boxes marked 1953, 1957, 1961—each filled with fedoras, pillboxes, and wide-brimmed sunhats that a Hollywood star would have found fetching. These were the heydays for hats and Roberto only sighs wearily when he thinks of all the unadorned heads nowadays.

He says that even though he worries about his craft, and acknowledges that he doubts a newly installed apprentice will carry on the 300-year-old continuity of his *botega*, Roberto says he wouldn't want to do anything else. Looking around the sawdust-covered workshop, small curls of limewood circling him as if he himself had just been released from a block of wood, he says, "Sometimes I am asked if I am a sculptor or an artisan. For me, a sculptor's life would be too difficult. You have to have your own ideas, and you always work alone." Roberto loves the feeling of camaraderie in the *botega*. "We always support each other," he says. He also could not work in any other medium. Metal and stone make him shudder. "The wood lives," he says as he caresses a curved surface that could be the shoulder of a friend but which is destined to become a broad-brimmed Panama hat. And with his cheeks glowing from the obvious passion he feels when he speaks of the softness and warmth of wood, he proudly pulls out a sketch which he says he has just received from Denmark. At the bottom is a royal seal. Roberto will soon carve a form for a hat that will sit atop the head of the Queen of Denmark.

While the atelier of the Beli brothers seems animated by the flow of sounds and laughter from the Piazza San Spirito, a few blocks away another workshop has the ambience of a surgical suite. Tucked behind two sets of doors, in a whitewashed and vaulted cavern where only the sound of some muffled Boccerini and the occasional rasp of metal on stone interrupt the palpable concentration, three artisans are bent inches from their work. This is a workshop where raw slices of stone are turned into what for all the world could be mistaken for subtly shaded and delicately drafted oil paintings. This is *pietre dure*, literally "hard stone" work, where intricate pictures are made using miniscule fragments of polished semiprecious stones.

While the Romans were the original masters of mosaic work and reveled in geometric patterns for floors and walls, it was the Florentine, Cosimo d'Medici, who in the late 14th century fell in love with the possibilities of *pietre dure*. His patronage of work that stretched from stony representations of flowers and birds, to battle scenes and portraits, made the artisanal craft a specialized Florentine art.

With light flooding into the workshop from an inner courtyard, Lucca Benotti, nearing 40, is gently rubbing two pieces of lapis lazuli together, literally massaging the stones into place. He has selected these two tiny shards for their color and striation—and for the picture his imagination is pulling out of the stone.

Lucca nods in the direction of some 40 drawers of raw rock: green malachite from Sudan, turquoise from the Cote d'Ivoire, quartz from the Congo. From Afghanistan, Turkey, Sweden, Chile, each slab carries colors and patterns to excite the artisans: greens, mauves, cerulean blue; swirls, waves, and dots and patterns that look like tiny trees and thunder storms. "If you're good at looking at a cloud and seeing sheep or demons or a wild horse, then you have some idea of the "inner eye" we use to select the exact centimeter of stone to, for instance, create a vein in an insect's wing or a wrinkle on an old man's face." Lucca speaks through a translator, but his reverence for this work is clear.

Nearby, another worker, Gabriel Asproni, who became an apprentice at 15 and who now, at 32, is working on a large reproduction of a prize beetle collection. He is getting ready to extract a match-size fragment from a slab of jade. Using a saw made from an arc of bamboo with a thin filament of steel holding the two ends taut, he saws into the stone two or three strokes, readjusts the stone, saws once or twice again, repeating this over and over until he has a tiny speckle to place upon a beetle's shell. He will glue the hundreds of stone pieces together upside down using hot beeswax, and when the beetle is complete, it will be inserted into the *intarsio,* the hole cut in the "background."

Both Lucca and Gabriel shrug when asked if it matters that their work is seemingly done in slow motion, given that Lucca's mountainous landscape, an 8 x 12-inch virtuoso piece, will take him over three months to complete. Although it will sell for thousands of dollars, money alone is not the motivator, they say. Like Roberto, the hat-form maker, who says he could never work in any other medium but wood, Lucca Benotti holds up a dull and dusty piece of stone. He takes a drop of oil and rubs it across the surface causing the rock to instantly come alive with color and depth and a strange transparency which reminds one of a Tuscan sunset. Then he holds it up with a smile. "These stones have stories to tell," he says. "I am here to release them."

Nearby, Carlo, older than the others, is evaluating some quartz "petals" in his hand. He feels optimistic, he says, about the future of *pietre dure*. He has just returned from Texas where he and a 17-year-old apprentice installed a colossal "Roman bath" with a diorama of gladiators at the Coliseum. The cost? The taciturn Carlo just laughs out loud. "For me," he says, "It is more about the love of these stones. I work every day. I teach every day. I learn every day." And how long does it take to become a true master of this craft? "Ah, Signora," he says, "The true answer is never!" With that, Carlo picks up a speck of yellow stone and gently adjusts it into a velvety blue sky—where one can almost see the star begin to twinkle.

This story was originally published in the St. Petersburg Times

Holy Ethiopia!

Smoky aviary filled with flowering blossoms and shrouded
smiles,
The chant of priests drifting like clouds across the Simien
peaks,
The march of cattle and goats, thin men's feet and the prance
of sheep
Turning the dusty road to a rumba floor, a do-si-do of chaos.

In the pages of Life Magazine, many years ago, a little American girl saw a photo of the coronation of Emperor Haile Selassie of Ethiopia—and an exotic seed was planted. Decades later, now a woman, she set out to learn about this ancient land.

**

The chant of a bearded priest drifts on the predawn air, ethereal, mysterious, all the ritual of Christianity's ancient Orthodox rites elaborated on his wavering harmonic.

I'm awake now, roused from a more primitive dream, one of the half-naked men and women I met yesterday—goat skins draped across their shoulders, cowry shells ringing their necks, 5-inch warthog tusks dangling from their ears. Sleepily, I wonder if it were real, until I finger the palm-size disc beside my bed, the one the Mursi girl had extracted from her split bottom lip and sold to me for a dollar.

Soon an ambulance siren on a Toyota van seems to bring the sun over the Mountains of Men and a catchy Amharic tune begins to drown out the priest and his repetitive good intentions. The

179

African city is awake, with its goats and sheep, smoky breakfast fires, and spill of sleepy, but smiling people.

This is Ethiopia—an amalgam, a confusion, a schizophrenic blending of cultures, centuries, peoples, and terrains. From the Semitic northerners with their exquisitely fine-featured beauty, where the elegance of the Queen of Sheba can still be seen in burnished skin and flowing ivory robes, to the tribal southerners, where nomadic cattle-tending, ritual scarring, and the unusual practice of powerful women begging men to beat them with sharpened whips—all allows Ethiopia to easily slip through one's grasp.

I traveled the country for one month, yet three months, perhaps three centuries would not be enough to truly understand this landlocked East African nation. Perched just above the equator and comprised of lake-dotted central highlands with four of Africa's highest peaks, and lowlands where acacia trees stretch across nearly barren savannahs, Ethiopia is nearly twice the size of Texas, with residents speaking 88 languages and hundreds of dialects. It is one of the poorest countries in Africa (average income is $400/year) and one of the most proud—a place where ancient history and modern life struggle for primacy.

As I sat, one afternoon, at the feet of a white-robed and turbaned priest in a rock church near Lalibela, the old man thumbed through an ancient text painted on goat skin. He described to me Ethiopia's glory days beginning when Sheba traveled to Israel to meet King Solomon. In a love at first sight scenario, the Queen begot a son who later returned to the land of Israel to meet his father, then brought back with him the Ark of the Covenant to Ethiopia. The old priest, leathery and smelling vaguely like the rock niche where he sleeps at night, points out that the Ark—"yes, the real Ark"—is kept under monastic guard in a special palace in Axum— never seen, but venerated as the touchstone of the country's fiercely Christian belief.

From ancient Axum to Lalibela, we traveled through the UNESCO World Heritage Site of the Simien Mountain National Park. In a 12-hour, bone-jarring journey through 13,000 ft. amethyst peaks and valleys carpeted in ribbons of flowering yellow meskel, we're accompanied by three "helpers"—powerful, robed men carrying AK-47s. Though I never learned exactly why 50-year-old "Muskula" was my seat partner, by the end of our day's journey, I barely noticed the metal barrel of his automatic rifle sticking up above his knees. But I had learned the Amharic words for, "I want a fish;" (for some reason) "I love you;" and, "*Babooshilada,*" the word for "baboon." "*Babooshilada, babooshilada,*" the old man winked at me as he disembarked. We were off to find one of the herds of wandering mountain Gelada primates. And with a wide grin, he'd lifted his AK in the air, waving goodbye as if it were a hankie and wishing me luck.

From Lalibela's eleven astounding 12th century churches carved from the top down into solid pink granite, we flew back to the capital, Addis Ababa, for the celebration of Meskel, the commemoration of the finding of the True Cross. Yes, in addition to having the Ark of the Covenant, Ethiopia also claims to have the "right arm" of the cross upon which Jesus was crucified, also under lock and key in a far-off monastery.

Meskel was all pageant: a parade of thousands of flag-waving faithful and hundreds of priests wearing gem-encrusted crowns under glittering robes in gumdrop colors. Gilded umbrellas kept the sun off elaborate golden crosses, and censers filled the air with the fragrance of frankincense. As night approached, the religiosity gave way to pure street dance, and nearly 800,000 people poured into the open air to shake their shoulders in the unique and exuberantly joyful of ethnic moves. Who could keep from joining them?

From Meskel, we headed south. Across the Great Rift Valley, where the earth's plates have violently pulled mountains apart. Past the signs of NGOs announcing their good works and infusions of money, beyond the ubiquitous, unfinished concrete buildings with their eucalyptus scaffolding, away from the massive conclaves of Chinese factory dormitories, and into what soon became a lawless, arid landscape peopled only by cattle, their teenaged herders, and bands of walkers, bent into question marks beneath breathtaking loads of fuel or forage.

These were the tribal lands of the Hamer people, the Mursi, the Karo, and Konso. Deep now in the Omo River Valley, we began to locate small clusters of mud and dung huts, their roofs in pointed thatch cones from which smoke rose like fog. With cinnamon-colored dirt and butter molding their complicated hairdos, the women emerged, babies on hips or backs, naked except for stretched skin skirts and copper coils around their arms. The men were tall and unsmiling. Many carried Kalashnikovs and had their bodies painted in geometric swirls of white clay. In a place where cattle constitute life itself, women's value is measured in a bride price of cows—up to 50 head for a beauty whose lip is stretched the size of a pancake.

Over the next days, we would watch Hamer women drink a potent corn brew until they were drunk enough to beg for whippings. We would see a young, naked man leap across the backs of nine cows in a rite of passage that readied him for marriage. And we would be taken aback as the so-called primitive inhabitants of each village struck poses worthy of Vogue models, then stuck out their hands sternly demanding "5 birr" (35 cents) for each photo. Who was corrupting whom became a question to be pondered.

And then it was over. For me, too soon. As the 16-hour plane ride became, thankfully, a fading memory, the past weeks began to settle back into their ancient past. With scratches of notes, and hundreds of photos, I looked at the small artifacts of Ethiopia I'd brought with me: a St. George's cross of hand-wrought silver, a white *shamma* shawl of woven cotton, a goatskin prayer book with small illuminations of the Annunciation, a lip plate, and a wooden pillow upon which a Karo herder once rested in a pasture.

I can't weave these items together, nor have them explain the land from which they've come. Rather, it is with a kind of relief that I realize that Ethiopia remains a mystery, obscured in the smoky morning fires of its history, indolent and beautiful, pious and pagan. It is a place I will not forget. Yet a place, like a tattered photo from Life, to forever ignite the imagination.

This story was originally published in the Tallahassee Democrat.

Marina Brown

Golden Bangles, Orange Moon, Swirling Scarlet Saris

Mahatma Gandhi. Ravi Shankar. Spicy curry and calming nan. More recently, *Eat, Love, Pray*—and the promise that a spiritual quest can lead to love.

Say "India," and these and a hundred more iconic images appear. But none of them can prepare a traveler, even a seasoned one, for India and its swirl of color, scents, throngs, and ancient archetypes that collide like brilliant molecules along the streets of Jaipur and Varanasi. Nor for women who, dazzling in golden bangles, march their oxen and swing their scythes in a desert's patch of green. Nor for crumbling palaces sprawling pink atop the hills, where monkeys play and peacocks wander, and the occasional tiger takes a nap.

But there is more. Years traveling in Tibet, China, Peru, and Greece, Egypt, Tunisia, Croatia, and scores of other exotic locations had always left me awed by civilization's burl-like configurations and the variations of religion and belief. Now, stepping into India was taking a dip into the strange spiritual soup with which this land has always nourished its peoples, its faiths, and its civilization in an oddly modulating synchrony. As a former churchgoer who'd studied Judaism when I was dating a Jew, the Koran for its poetry, and Buddhism as far as Herman Hesse, spirituality seemed a part of my life, while religion's formal side no longer was. In India however, it seemed faith was the *nan* of life.

So what is it that *makes up* the "real India"—both its colorful here and now, and its ethereal heart? I wanted to know, but like the blind men describing an elephant—the one near the trunk describing a thin animal with a long neck, the one on its back insisting it has a hump like a camel's—a visitor's impression of an entire subcontinent is bound to be limited by his or her own tiny perspective.

Mine, however, was of a particularly rich section of India: Delhi, Jaipur, Khajuraho, Agra, Varanasi—the cities of the state of Rajasthan, where the Hindu gods presided over the Indus valley 4000 years ago. This is where Siddhartha had two great religions, Buddhism and Jainism, created in his name; and where the Muslim Mughal emperors ruled for the last thousand years until their defeat by the British two hundred years ago. Each religion has brought a cosmology, a cuisine, a culture, a promise. And the remarkable fact about India is that these diverse views have somehow become woven into the intricate and dramatic brocade that is embraced by all Indians, no matter what the religion they practice.

My introduction to that sumptuous fabric was on my first day in Old Delhi—the capital before the British took control. With a garland of moist marigolds around my neck and a red paste *bindi* popped between my eyes by a Hindu girl smiling a welcome, I was now bouncing in a rickshaw along the narrow alleys of Chandi Chowk's bazaar. First came the chicken merchants, then the curry vendors, and finally the kinetic cacophony of the peacock fan and sari sellers. At my fingertips the city flowed: men with orange-hennaed hair, women with thick black braids and arms covered by twinkling bracelets. massive blue turbans above fluffy black beards. and some of the most spectacularly disfigured beggars imaginable. We wove; we paused; but my three-wheeled rickshaw never stopped despite the humanity, the sacred cows, the wandering pigs, and serenely oncoming cars. I loved it. I marveled at the lack of acrimony: no jostling, no road rage. Rather, a collegial braiding of motion, as if people and vehicles were improvising to a tune each one could hear.

Later, at the famed Jama Mosque, the guardian of the reliquary produced a seldom-seen object of veneration: one delicate hair, mounted vertically inside a crystal cylinder, said to be a hair from the beard of the Prophet, and an ancient sandal buried in yellowed petals, that He once wore. I knelt inches from the little hair—my mind balanced between easy dismissal of a questionable relic, and jaw-dropping awe that such a tiny organic fragment could bring me within inches of One who had changed a third of the world. Soon the call to prayer of the *muezzin* began to echo across the courtyard, creating a resonating chord within each listener. I could appreciate the depth of the Muslims' belief.

Hours later, at the Raj Ghat, the memorial site of Mahatma Gandhi's cremation, along with others, I circled a small fountain five times, thinking deeply of the great Hindu's vision for his country—peaceful, non-confrontational, filled with the same precepts as in Buddhism— and detached from the trappings of the world. Just as I was thinking that we needed more of that, I tripped over a street vendor's wares. But it was not a white-robed aesthetic who offered a hand, but a corpulent Sikh, swathed in a brilliant red turban with an expensive gold watch. He jovially pretended to dust me off, then gave a little bow and a prayer-handed "Namaste"—the god in him greeting the god in me. I happily reciprocated, beginning not to feel like a tourist, but like another spinning molecule in the happy diversity around me.

**

To the south, the city of Jaipur is perhaps the most majesty-filled city of India, redolent with palaces, forts, and pleasure-houses, all of a uniquely pink sandstone covered in ornamental scrolls. The famed *zenana*, or women's quarters, soars above the street with hundreds of tiny latticed windows, looking for all the world, like a stage set for Arabian Nights. Even though the maharajas were Hindu, the Muslim practice of women's seclusion was maintained until around the Second World War. Still today, Hindu women often pull a sari's end across their faces, probably never noting their nod to women of another faith.

But, as India is home to the Kama Sutra and the erotic carvings at Khajuraho, some things were purely secular. Especially in the heyday of the Maharajas. For centuries in Rajasthan, some of the wealthiest of these nobles had accumulated bounty from taxing the caravans along the Silk Road and imposing heavy taxes on their subjects.

In 1947, before all the princes voluntarily gave over their estates to the nascent nation of India, the dichotomy between their benevolence and their consumption was astounding. Each year, most maharajas distributed their weight in silver to the poor, but they also were holding recreational elephant fights and shooting game as if swatting flies. In Chooch Behar, the maharaja shot 365 tigers, 311 leopards, 207 rhinos, and 211 bears during his lengthy reign. Today, their titles rescinded by the government, the descendants of these princely families have been forced to turn their palaces into resorts or hotels, or give them to the government as museums.

Further south was the Ranthambore Tiger Reserve, formerly hunting lands for a maharaja's clan, where I stayed at the Nahargarh Hotel. "Hotel" is a misnomer. Created in the guise of his family's 16th century palace, the descendant of the Thakur of Alsisar has made a walled fortress comprised of four courtyards, hundreds of mirrored and plaster-carved rooms, pools, fountains, arcades, and cupolaed spots for rendezvous. A red-coated musician wanders among the candlelit tables of a flower-filled courtyard, singing for diners who sip white wine, and who will later marvel at an orange moon rising through trellised roses. Ah, the perfumed life, the sensual sensory input.... Tiger sightings, monkey pranks, and surrounded by enough wild peacocks to start a farm, I found myself indulgently missing the life of the maharajas probably as much as they do.

**

Agra, as evident as was the Taj Mahal's beauty, for me, remained cool, hard and perfect, the mausoleum's marble symmetry fossilized into a postcard archetype. Instead, it was the dirty pandemonium of the city of Varanasi that again gave life to India's soul. I heard it speaking each night from atop the minarets and in the echoes of the temple's conchs.

Scattered along the *ghats*, the steep steps leading to the Ganges, Varanasi's purpose is evident. Here, in the sacred river, the faithful, sit, stand, wade, wash, pray, sing, weep, and have a good shave. A holy man smears a *bindi* onto my forehead, but waves off a tip. An old woman holds up a dripping baby for me to admire, its wide eyes ringed with kohl. Young boys are draped in orange yoga robes. A man in white stands with hands clasped in prayer.

Nearby, a group with shaved heads has just cremated a loved one—only steps away from old women having a bath. This is a place where at any one time, over 20 funeral pyres burn brightly beside the sacred river. The sanctity of the Ganges, for these people, cannot be denied. Their relationship with what is holy—their river, in their acts of kindness, in their acceptance of what is—is something I have seen flow within each person I have met, no matter their religion, no matter their caste.

The rural farmer living in a reed house beside a stream, when asked if he could change three things about his life, only smiled, shrugged, and after many long moments said, "...maybe a refrigerator...." The gypsy child with matted hair and dirty legs who brings me a marigold and a hug. The leper woman with no hands, who assures me her life is good and she would not exchange it with anyone. All of these moments make me think I have seen how faith of all kinds brings peace to a people. I say this as I, too, find comfort—in packing into my suitcase a dried leaf dropped from the tree under which, it is said, the Buddha received Enlightenment. What does it mean? Perhaps only that I will have a decaying souvenir. Perhaps more.

And so, I leave India, able to speak of it truly only in metaphor. Like trees in a forest, crowded, but amiable, each bends a bit to allow light from above to fall onto another. Thus, I found the accommodating religions and practices of this ancient land, like the guises of the Hindu gods, each one an aspect of personality or of need. India can be many things to many people—changing always, but ever, ever itself.

This story was originally published in the Tallahassee Democrat.

My Ghost

The first time I had come to Puycelsi, a tiny hilltop hamlet in the southerly middle of France, I was a young mother of three school-age children. My then-husband was a professor who shared teaching responsibilities with a French counterpart which allowed each family to spend summers in the other's country. Puycelsi had been chosen almost at random for our first sojourn, mostly because of its pastoral location in the rolling farmland of the Occitanie. There, the countryside is filled with caves and rivers, with the history of small warring duchies on their tumultuous journey to becoming *France,* and it is also chock-full of archeological sites where ancient hominids ran mammoths off cliffs. Besides, Puycelsi, one on a circuit of small, walled fortresses called *bastides,* looked for all the world like my storybook version of where princesses got rescued from dragons.

Now, children grown, the professor deceased, I wanted to show my new husband this medieval dreamscape—the repository of years of memories filled with summer hollyhocks and ancient stones. And ghosts.

Okay. Let's be honest. Coming back to Puycelsi probably had everything to do with the ghost—the sad young man who it was said, lived in the house we always rented. Through the centuries he'd lingered there, awaiting his execution—somehow stranded in an upstairs bedroom of the inn. Others had seen the youth. I'd certainly felt him. I wondered if after 40 years he were still there. Then again, he'd been around Puycelsi, this 12th century French village since the 1700s—why would he get up and leave now? After all of these years, I longed to find out.

Of course, France had changed since my long-ago summers. Other French towns to the south, impressive ones like Carcassonne, with its massive castle, and Albi, with its sky-filling cathedral, remained magnificent. But as we wound our way north, poor towns the color of soiled manila, squatted beside the road. Nomad's encampments sprawled next to glorious turret-topped forts. Women in abayas, tomatoes directly from heaven, African sellers of sunglasses, and strutting geese willing to sacrifice their livers for foie gras as silky as grease—all are a part of the paradoxical landscape of Southern France today.

Yet as we came closer to Puycelsi, things seemed simpler. The region is called Languedoc, relating to the language of the *"Occitane"* that was once spoken here. It is the region where blues and ochres seem to take on new life; where fields of sunflowers track the hours, obediently tilting their heads with the passage of light; and where chartreuse vineyards with fat gold grapes lie beside perfumed plots of lavender—all of it forming a heady quilt draped across the hips and shoulders of the red clay of the Tarn valley.

This land and Puycelsi had spoken to me from the start. I'd known a man from Arkansas, who, when he first saw Japan, wept and said he'd "come home." And a Brit who'd settled in Marrakesh who said that her soul had always lived there—it was only that she'd had to find it. In some ways, that's how I'd thought about Puycelsi from that first moment when the towers and turrets had materialized above encircling mists that surround the crenelated pinnacle. I'm not really a Francophile, though I speak the language and like the food. But Bastille Day is not, for me, a major holiday. Still, the heart knows its home, and this far-away village had kept me a loyal lover down through the years. I only wondered if, as lovers do, it had changed.

Miraculously, the house we had rented in the village 40 years before, was today, still an auberge. In the 12th century, the three-story stone house had been a garrison, hosting soldiers from one of the many wars between the Counts of Toulouse, the Knights

Templar, and the King of France. There, while my children had played hide and seek through the village and held snail races on our front step, I could hear the meat vendor calling his wares, look from my kitchen at the stone mason repointing stones of the mayor's house, and watch the old men, one hand behind their back, throwing the metal *petanque* ball toward a wooden nut in the churchyard. It was as it might always have been, intimate, charming—not a reenactment, but a kind of medieval life actually being lived. I hoped it had not all disappeared.

Now, hand in hand with my husband, as we walked down the lanes of the tiny walled village, filled one moment with sunlight, and the next with violet shadows, memories came flooding back. I began to see that Puycelsi was even more beautiful than I had remembered—more beautiful than it had been four decades earlier.

A path now circled the village, following the course of the ramparts where gardens next to half-timbered houses were filled with fig trees and flowers. Instead of one small restaurant, there were now three, each of them with views across the land towards the Cevennes and the Alps beyond. The houses that had, through the centuries variously been inhabited, or abandoned and fallen into disrepair, were now curtained with lace, adorned with geraniums and graced with cats, all supremely diffident, as French cats are. Yet tourists could be counted on one hand. It was perfect.

I wandered down to the square, listening to the soft sounds of a choir rehearsing in the church for a memorial to the dead of the First War. At an angle in the ramparts is a well, covered now, but the place where an old lady with tears in her eyes had once told me how 850 years earlier the Crusaders stormed the village, casting into the well the Christian Cathars who prayed in a different way than the Roman Pope, and who were therefore branded heretics. She had taken me by the hand to a small stone cottage and shown me where a few lucky Cathars had escaped through a rocky passage hewn into the rock from beneath the cattle stall inside the little house. The old lady, as do many who live close to the land and perhaps closer to its history, still mourned them.

Though I can't say I mourned for my remembered ghost, I too, in a way, had lived with his memory for many years. With my return, I hoped I would find out if he were still there.

The ghost had appeared to many. In fact, in the winter months when Puycelsi grows cold and dark and the winds claw at the windows, caretakers admit they simply don't go into some buildings. "*Plein d' esprits*," "full of spirits," they'd say. Our house was one.

Years ago, one guest recalled his encounter in detail. As he'd mounted the stone steps to an upstairs mezzanine, there, reclining on a chaise was a distraught and weeping youth. "He wore period clothes... as if from Napoleon's time," Dalton Robertson, a Canadian journalist, had said. "I have never felt such a flood of sadness." Over time, others had met the young man, who apparently was awaiting his execution in the square outside. The then-owner of the house admitted she rarely went to that second level— "especially one room," she'd said cryptically.

But I had. A tiny room adjoining the mezzanine seemed to be the place she avoided, and opening its door, I couldn't imagine why. There was a bedcover of red and white checks and two Gothic-tipped windows flanked by stone seats that suggested a medieval lady of status may have found it an inviting place to read or sew. I had lightly touched the patinaed armoire and the carved walls, and I noted how the light turned red and green through tiny stained-glass scenes of a hunt. It was beautiful and I took out my camera to record the charm of the place, but no sooner had I begun snapping photos, than a "thickness" filled the room. It was a singular feeling of oppression and despair, so heavy that I felt I couldn't breathe, as if I would have to part the air to escape. This very, very definitely felt like an invitation to leave. That was what I remembered most, that the presence in the room had wanted me out.

Now, the new owners of the lovely, "refurbished" auberge, when pressed, seem casual, if cagey, about "the ghost." "He doesn't come here anymore," I was told with averted eyes. "Renovations have been made. Walls have been moved." But as I wandered from a new guest quarters added to "our" old house, I could see that the interior of the ancient garrison was still just as it had been. The stone steps led directly up to the "room", just as they always had. The mezzanine, where the youth had reclined, still retained a view of the square where he was later hanged. And though the owners say an elderly relative now lives on that private level and cannot be disturbed, he is never seen, never heard, and never makes a request.

Just as my ghost might, I think. Though in truth, "my" ghost never belonged just to me. And to be honest, I don't think he even liked me!

This story was originally published in the Tallahassee Democrat.

All Through the Night

The last rumbles from the third storm to tear through Tallahassee are still growling their way toward Georgia when I arrive at Broderick Vaughan's rural operation. As I bounce along the property's dirt path, friendly chickens and guinea hens cluck "hello" in the fading light. A couple of dogs stand around sniffing at the 20-ft airboat riding high on its trailer near the processing building and cool shed.

Things seem quiet, even tranquil here, until the rail-thin dynamo that is Broderick Vaughan appears from a shed. Vaughan was a roofer for 25 years, until in 2010, he gave up roofing and began concentrating on establishing a business doing what he really loves—hunting alligators and guiding others to do it too.

Tonight, we are preparing to go out on what Vaughn promises to be a true Florida adventure, a watery "safari" of sorts, where man will stalk a primordial reptile, then be home to watch The Tonight Show by eleven. But just now, Vaughn is jumping on and off the trailered-airboat, organizing poles with grapple hooks, bang sticks, and a 20 pound-plus crossbow he describes as having been used to take 150 nuisance alligators last year "from just about any place alligators and people meet up without wanting to." That includes, lakes, ponds, swimming pools, golf courses, and even in the middle of roads. Despite the dangers inherent in securing and removing animals that can weigh nearly 1000 pounds and fight with claws, teeth, and tail, Vaughan receives only $30 per alligator trapped.

"Trappers are permitted to keep the hides and meat from the gators they remove," he says. That means weighing, skinning, processing and preparing the meat for sale and the hides for tanning. It's enough to make a living.

Vaughan sweeps his hand toward his new processing barn. It's a state-of-the-art facility with two powerfully built stainless steel tables—akin to autopsy tables on CSI. That's where alligators will continue their lives as purses and belts, or where, as do hogs and fowl, they will provide meat for the tables of those who follow the hunting tradition.

Outside, Vaughan hops onto the airboat, a relatively new purchase, and tests the motor with a monolithic roar. He's added some headlamps, and several tarmac-ready ear protectors to our gear, and before we launch, he politely asks if anybody needs to use the facility. "We may be out for a while," he says. A sentence filled, we discover, with underestimation.

In the meantime, we take a peek inside a "cold-shed," which is at first a blissful respite from the evening swelter. Then, its distinctive aroma washes over us. A huge plastic bin holds the bumpy skins of two recently slaughtered alligators. The corner contains the decapitated heads of six others, smiling skyward in order of size. On the floor is a large 9-footer, spread-eagle (uh…reptile) on its back and two smaller gators, only one of which is dead. "We've got its mouth still taped," says Vaughan, "and the cold will keep him nice and quiet until he goes to the processing room.

Tonight's licensed alligator hunter is Tom Udell, a friend of Vaughan's who has hunted alligators for five years. His license, one of 5,000 issued this year from 10,000 applications, will allow him to take two animals during his designated one week First Phase of the four weekly Phases. If he fails to get two alligators, he will be allowed to try again during the last "open" Phase from September to November. Udell has already gotten one and plans on tonight tagging his second. "Lake Miccosukee is full of 'um," he says.

And there's another passenger in the airboat: Vaughan's just-turned 15-year-old daughter, Kelvy. Picture a 5'9", long-haired, Twiggy look-alike, who instead of trying to choose between future professions of radiology assistant or professional alligator trapper, could be on a Paris runway. The girl, despite her striking looks, is her father's daughter. With classic Southern manners, and each question answered with a "Ma'am" or "Sir", Kelvy says she loves alligator hunting, having shot her first gator when she was nine. Kelvy will become our guide as her father and Udell focus on the slow business of stalking reptiles, who very definitely do not want to become handbags.

Eight PM: The airboat is eased into Lake Miccosukee, a 6312-acre prairie lake that in 10-year cycles empties into a sink hole which in turn feeds the Florida Aquifer. A spillway was built in 1954 that allows the lake level to be controlled, and like Lake Jackson, to be emptied from time to time. Currently, carpets of water lilies, hydrilla, and tuffets of grass seem to choke parts of the lake, but Vaughan's airboat will ride over and through them. The night air is soft and wet, and with cypress trees rising out of chrome-colored water, the tangerine streaks of lightning in the eastern sky make the moment magical.

"There's an 11-footer just swimmin' off the dock," calls a man with feet outstretched, watching the moon rise from his chair. "Best place to git one might be right here...." Prophets, it seems, walk the land.

Vaughan turns on the engine once everyone is ensconced, and we tear off to a far side of the lake where he and Udell have seen "some big ones."

Nine PM: Vaughan and Udell have donned headlamps. As they turn their heads back and forth, the water is strafed with beams of light, crossing, crisscrossing, illuminating the shoreline and flat, plate-sized lily pads, looking for the telltale red glow of an alligator eye peering at us above the surface. Half an hour goes by with light from only their headlamps and the haloed quarter moon—but not one eye to be seen. And then, from the bow of the boat, a burst of whispered excitement.

Quietly, Udell picks up the crossbow, mounts it against his shoulder, focusing its aiming light on a red watery eye. Vaughan allows the motor of the airboat to go silent and with a small electric trolling motor sporadically moving us forward, heads directly for the "neon" pupil. We ghost down on the alligator. Udell is standing up, essentially drifting to within feet of what might be "at least an 8-footer," when what will happen throughout the night occurs. Nothing. The gator sensing an ominous shadow, a suspicious sound, or the scent of murder—disappears without a ripple beneath the surface. Udell lowers his bow. It's not called a hunt for nothing.

10 PM: The moon has risen, peaked, and now having turned everything a dusky cream, is slowing sinking west. We drift through the grassy labyrinth, which is as confusing as the delta in *African Queen*, while the lake seems to give off the light note of funeral home flowers. Vaughan and Udell stand side by side on the flat surface of the bow, silhouetted like warriors, alert for the slightest movement or a drift of red in the dark water below us.

But if the alligators aren't in the mood, everything else is. Bats are streaking by like large butterflies, buzzing the boat and taking advantage of the circles of illuminated insects that halo the men's heads. Frogs are making themselves hoarse with high clicks, low thumps, and once Kelvy asks her father if she hears coyotes barking in the distance. He affirms that indeed she does.

The hour passes. Then another. Three times eyes are seen. As if taking no chance of a spooked gator at close range, Vaughan has cast his three-pronged grapple hook from a rod, hoping to snag a gator, haul it close, and enable Udell to shoot it with his harpoon from the bow. Three times, and by the end of the expedition, a dozen, the hook is retrieved from the water with only wet flora and the ripples of a diving gator to show for it.

2AM: Vaughan is now not only making alligator sounds of his own—little noises that are like, "Ow!" into a coffee cup—but now he has turned on the recorded voices of baby alligators and their big bull daddies hoping perhaps to lure worried mothers or feisty males our way. The baby alligator noises are sweet—something between a wet smooch and an old Pac Man video game. While the males call out in a breathy bellow.

"This might be the way to get a 10-footer," he suggests. "Alligators have small brains, but they use all of 'um." That they do. Time and again a set of eyes has dropped below the surface, easily eluding Udell's crossbow, which he's now begun to complain feels "like a ton."

4AM: Teenage Kelvy, who has not whined once since the evening started, has however, been asleep for several hours. For the rest of us, it feels as if the lake is playing tricks. Pods of grass are masquerading as sleeping gators, while the real ones slip under the floating islands of Miccosukee grass. A "magic tree" appears white in someone's headlamp, daubed with silvery spectres that suddenly flap their wings and fly away with a curse. Here and there, what looks like a large Brussels sprout, stands alone on a platinum plate. We are very tired.

Somewhere around 4:30 AM the bulb on Udell's headlamp burns out, and soon the batteries for his crossbow light are gone. Broderick Vaughan is the only one who continues to hop from airboat engine to small troller motor, scanning the shore like a hyperactive wading bird with the patience of Job. In a last-ditch effort to come back with a gator, he heads us into a stand of cypress, grey, thick, dripping with moss—a scene from a horror movie— when suddenly a massive form lurches from beneath a tree—6 ft away and into the water. The Big One—maybe a 12-footer. No, definitely a 12-footer. Could have been 13. Now swimming happily away.

5 AM: There have been shots taken. Twice Udell aimed and fired at the surfaced dorsal-half of a gator. The first time the harpoon ricocheted off the animal's back; the second, Vaughan says it hit the gator's "face," but bounced off the bony head. "You know, we usually don't go in till we come back with somethin'," he says apologetically. It seems Vaughan would be happy to hunt through till 10am when the hunting hours close, but perhaps a second look at his drowsy daughter and the muscle-weary Udell tell him that for tonight, the gators have come out on top.

As we step out of the boat, the men trade platitudes common to hunters: "We should'a gotten that 11-footer right out here by the dock," says Udell. "Them big ones been around for what…25 years…hard to put much over on 'um." And finally, "Well, the really big ones will be around in November, that's the best time to get the really crafty ones…. Yeah, we'll get one big-ass gator then…."

Already the sound of stirring shore birds stretching out wings and giving preliminary squawks can be heard. The sky has turned pale in the east. And on this new day, perhaps some gator will stretch out in the sun, catch himself a fish, and marvel at the odd goings-on in his peaceful neighborhood last night. We hope he's not thinking about November.

This story was originally published in the Tallahassee Democrat.

Italy Is Where...

Firenze

Where from a busy restaurant, an aunt carries out a bowl of thick soup the chef has just insisted she take for free. On the sidewalk, the mother dips a spoon in the bowl of green porridge and places mouthfuls of loving sustenance first on one baby's smacking lips, then the other's. The aunt holds the soup, the grandmother wipes the two tiny mouths, the father, grandpa, and uncle, all bend over the scene—soldiers on call for assistance.

*

Where you find that at the end of a meal, the waitress and the patrons grasp each other's shoulders and give double-cheeked kisses, then following fervent words of affection, they respectively blow kisses toward one another from across the street.

*

Where there are exhausted climbers of cathedral steps, and museum stairs, and vertical inclines that leave aging tour group ladies bent over stone bannisters heaving 20-pound bosoms up and down with such exhausted force that they themselves resemble little symbols of America—with their blue lips, crimson cheeks, and white dandelion hair blowing in the autumn breeze.

*

Where with the soft golden-blue of a Florence twilight, the first sounds begin: a faraway rumble as if the city is gently clearing its throat. Then a pulsing, a quickening, no longer organic, but brutally

201

metallic—suggesting that that "scissors" will win over "rock." It's the beginning of the evening's goodbye to conversation—later to a night of sleep. Where wheelbarrows and carts and wooden trolleys filled with the market's unsaleable leather goods will twice a day take a caravan ride along uneven granite cobbles from the storage garage beneath our house to the market—and lest we worry—back again.

But do we fret? Of course not. By two AM, it will be over. And tomorrow's six AM rumblings not yet begun.

*

Where you sit down in a tiny osteria that under the watchful eye of "*nonna* Olga," uses recipes begun a generation ago. And just as the *scallopini* arrives and the *porcini* and sausage starter have disappeared, a crowd of people enter the tiny restaurant. It's a celebration of a graduation from pharmacy school. A *Dottore* now, the Laureate enters wearing a corona of laurel leaves tied with a red bow. Smiling until his face breaks, "Lorenzo" is toasted by friends and sung to by his grandpa, who's had to literally be carried to his chair for the occasion.

Then, after I pass a little portrait to the graduate with good wishes for his future, the whole table erupts with applause for the napkin sketch, along with offers of wine and *torte*. As family members "ooh and ah," they assure me the "masterpiece," the yellow napkin portrait, will be framed and hung in the salon *subito*!

*

Where you go to buy two peppers at the tiny *mercato*, and the grocer, Alberto, throws in another for free—because he likes our conversation.

*

Where the moment it rains, dozens of perfectly healthy dogs on leashes are whisked into their owners' arms and carried beneath umbrellas in frontal pouches like infants. Others who ride in strollers have the "shade" dropped so not a drop will touch their thick and pampered coats. Other luckier dogs just huddle inside the purses their owners carry them in—little wombs from which they only rarely emerge.

*

Where from my tiny terrazzo, circled by red begonias, yellow pansies, lavender, and bright orange zinnias, I peek at a square of sky as blue as an evil eye. On this red terra cotta terrace with its tall green shutters and delicate table and chair, I am a *Principessa*, protected by iron works that curl like tendrils to reveal only a reality censored for my delicate sensibilities.

Still, a metal gutter spills moldy water from the chicken-wired patio above. Five plumbing pipes, each capped to hold down the methane's release stand proudly side by side. Peeling plaster in abstract Pollock-patterns highlight the greened cement below, and the brick wall that crumbles mortar at my feet slumps against the asphalt swirls that have pasted it into place. The sagging cornices, the eves that are tacked on by wires that themselves hang loose, and the Escher-angles of roofs and walls and stairs built and pulled down and made again above a door that was itself moved twice— are all a testament to make-do, to innovation, to Beauty of a kind, a barely functioning function of Italians' desire to live in a city too small for too many—yet elegant in its demise. Just as the ravaged beauty of a Donatella or a Francesca, eyes circled with age, Florence still tries for one last romance.

Napoli

Where the people are either terribly ill or incredibly clumsy, judging by the number of screaming ambulances that daily plow through traffic, and where red lights are suggestions, and broken-field motorbike-riding, preferably veering across the white dividing line, is the norm. Where making U-turns in busy traffic into the two lanes of bumper-to-bumper traffic is expected. Where suicidal pedestrians simply step off curbs into oncoming buses, motorcycles, ambulances, bikes, and trucks that obligingly stop for them without a word and even swerve for their night-time silhouettes—and never receive a horn-blow.

*

Where old men walk alone, heads down, arms folded behind them, often wearing caps and little cotton vests. Where their now solitary apartments have grown too filled with memories, and they stroll and sit, wishing for an Agnes or a Filomena to stroll and sit with—and how arm in arm is better than two hands clasped behind you.

*

Where laundry hangs from even grand turn-of-the-century apartments, revealing the owners' taste in pajamas, colorful sheets, a preference for striped boxers, and the size of grandma's bust. Where we can learn that Sergio has moved back home by his bright yellow jeans flapping in the sun, and that Sophia finally delivered the overdue baby by the tiny flags sporting Teddy bears and Fairies. And where the absence of Gino's underwear says all we need to know about Maria's temper outbursts and the fact that we can see his jockeys now drying in the sun at Teresa's.

*

Where Neapolitans have somehow developed a tolerance for graffiti and the ability to ignore masses of recycled garbage that spill from the megalithic yellow, grey, and blue bins adorning every 17th century building's entrance. Where the graffiti Americans would call "gang tagging" spreads like colorful algae on store fronts, federal buildings, train stations, bridges, and even churches, and which Neapolitans see as "expressive creativity." Where, in fact, once you get used to it, graffiti stretching two-stories high and placed next to 9 or 10 shoulder-high recycling bins that overflow their garbage, metal, plastics and paper into obsessively recycled mountains of blue-bagged refuse—once you're really used to it, you'll find that the two pair together quite nicely. Graffiti and garbage. Even the aroma is similar.

*

Where ochre-toned palazzos, once the homes of well-to-do merchants and vendors, perhaps clothiers to Dukes and Duchesses, or pretenders to Neapolitan thrones, have crumbled now into apartment walk-ups, each with a groin-vaulted vestibule and a niche for a statue of great uncle Aldo—who absconded to Malta with the neighbor's swarthy, but buxom maid. Where the foyer is now only for the dented Fiat and laundry supplies; for 13 bicycles, four baby carriages, and a rusted Vespa cowering beneath a blue plastic tarp. Yet the marble steps ascend, their bannisters carved in voluptuous curves, where each landing forms a platform to meticulously observe the fractured plaster, the cracked sills, the deep gouges for wires and plumbing and a satellite dish's perch—that have ingloriously allowed this ravaged building to survive a wrecking ball or a squatter's fire. And though quietly raped of her beauty, this once grande dame still stands.

*

Where thick-necked men in groaningly tight T-shirts gather to breathe-in the testosterone that rises in pheromone fog around them. They don't seem interested in the women here—some glamorous beauties with medusa hair and olive skin—some haggard blondes, caked with eyeliner not removed all week. Instead, the men engage each other, louder and louder, sentences shouted over another man's words, arms in spirals, fingers unfurling like time-lapsed blossoms. There is anger here, intimidation for sure. Yet they stroke each other's shoulders and caress each other's cheeks, and you wonder if the hit will happen in the restaurant or on the street, and if the soon-to-be widow has her black silk stockings all picked out.

Marina Brown

Sorrento

Where there is fragrance of a time gone by, elegant old hotels with iron staircases and bannisters of metal vines. Where the feeling that one may meet a character on the terrace from a Noel Coward play, where the emanations of a First and a Second War linger in air wafted from a hillside lemon grove, and where the soft music of Schumann or Caruso's songs can be heard through tall, laced windows overlooking the sea.

*

Sorrento, this place of suspended time, where Brahms came, and Wagner, and Oscar Wilde, the last exotic stop on the Grand Tour for wealthy youth and debutantes—a place where homosexuals could be themselves, where English dowagers could watch clouds drift above Capri and pretend that they were not pretending.

*

Sorrento, where you wish your companion carried a walking stick and you wore strands of pearls, that the *ristorante*'s waiter offered Verdi with prosecco in long thin flutes, where you hope the ring of jewels of Naples won't stop sparkling across the Bay, and Vesuvius will mind her manners on this pastel afternoon.

*

Sorrento, where on the way to the train station, pulling suitcases and carrying hand luggage, the umbrella stuffed deeply inside the valise as if it were a beloved family jewel the pickpockets had been watching for days, the squall hits.

At the waterfront in Sorrento, the wind tears down the mountainsides, pulling bits of Vesuvius along with it, while in a Trumpian tantrum, the Bay of Naples hurls in half its contents toward the shore. I walk on, generally demonstrating how to bathe with your clothes on in the shower while holding luggage and

206

attempting to force open a Chinese-made umbrella that is obviously part of a Sino-American power struggle—and the Chinese win.

Since there are no taxis—they've taken the day off— I crouch in the storm between two vehicles, one a beaten-up yellow bus— when its kindly driver opens his door and politely invites me in. I'm the only one there. He's not on duty. Not due to move for an hour. Nor is the train station on his route. But when he finds that's my destination, he simply says, "*Andiamo*." And off we go. A private ride, not on his route, a little gift from a gentle, taciturn Sorrentino. No ticket, no payment—just a kindness to a fellow traveler in life. After all, we've all found ourselves caught in a storm.

*

Where today in Sorrento, I saw a photo of a woman, an old woman, her still thick grey hair in a braided bun at the base of her neck. We see only her back as she sits on high rocks overlooking the Bay of Naples and Capri. She remains slim, but you see the weathered skin of her hands and arms. She gazes across the water. She is still. Perhaps for hours her reverie has held her, unmoving, except for the memories of long ago, when the wavy grey hair was black, and she lay along these rocks, caressed by a young man— perhaps later, another who loved her more. Perhaps she hears the laughter of other lovers from across the Bay, from a swirling evening of waltzing along the edge of Capri.

The loves, the losses, the war, the beginnings, the endings, the girl she was. The girl she was. A moment in the scheme of things, a moment along these rocks that alone with her, hold the secrets of a youth that was gone too soon. And yet, she lived the moments, she wasted little. And so, this hour, when the ghosts return to again caress her in the sun, must not be wasted. Nor the tears.

Nor the tears.

About the Author

Marina Brown has written for newspapers and magazines for the last 20 years, including the St. Petersburg Times, the Tallahassee Democrat, Florida Design, and Dance Magazine. She is the recipient of numerous national writing awards: two First Place awards in the Porter Fleming Short Story Contest, Second Place in the Lorian Hemingway Contest for Short Stories, First Place in the Red Hills Poetry Contest, and she received the Florida Authors and Publishers Association (FAPA) Silver Medal for her poetry volume, *The Leaf Does Not Believe It Will Fall.* In 2020, Brown was nominated for the State of Florida Poet Laureate.

Brown's novels, *Land Without Mirrors* (2013) and *Lisbeth* (2017) both won Gold Medals in Literary Fiction from the FAPA. Her most recent work of Historical Fiction, *The Orphan of Pitigliano*, won the Florida Writers Association's Royal Palm Literary Awards' Gold Medal as well as the top award, the 2020 Book of the Year.

Brown is a former professional ballet dancer, a sailor, a watercolorist, a cellist, and a traveler. She lives in Tallahassee.

Contact Marina Brown at mcdb100@comcast.net for signings, readings, or book club appearances.

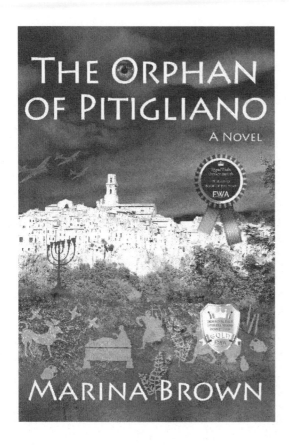

Scan to buy on Amazon

GOLD MEDAL AND BOOK of the YEAR - RPLA

As the Nazis menace Italy in 1938, 17-year-old Giuliana and her two cousins flee to Pitigliano, a 13th century Tuscan hill town, to conceal their Jewish identity. Amidst tragedy, Giuliana finds love, as well as strange dangers far greater than the Nazi threat.

The treasures of an Etruscan tomb, an unholy perversion, and above all, *"il malocchio"*—the Evil Eye—tear the cousins apart.

Now, 30 years later, Giuliana lies in a sleep-like trance in Boston, felled by *il malocchio* and a jealousy that will not die.

The Orphan of Pitigliano is a love story that persists beyond the malevolent "gaze" in a sweeping panorama of Italy and secrets of three generations who each think of themselves as "orphans."

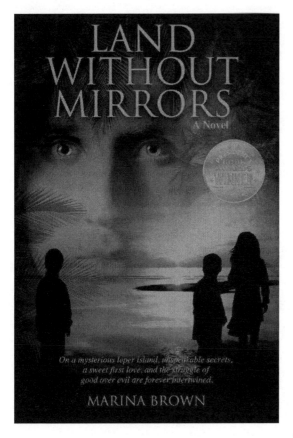

Scan to buy on Amazon

"Can I feel my fingertips? Am I one of them now?"

Brown's Gold Medal-winning, debut novel is set on an exotic Caribbean island inhabited solely by exiled lepers and their caregivers. Here, a sinister priest, an enigmatic nun, and a troubled doctor engage in a dangerous struggle for power, as three youths yearn for a different life, wondering if they too are diseased.

Even as the intense search for a cure for leprosy washes throughout the tale, *Land Without Mirrors* is at heart a love story—mothers for their children; men for power and fame; and a sweet first love that grows to maturity.

Scan to buy on Amazon

"There's killin' goin' on tonight…" Lisbeth wept. And in response to the young man's surprise, she whispered, "I think I killed my father… and my father has certainly killed me."

So begins the intriguing Gothic saga that leaps time and place as two families - one black, one white - discover their shared need for retribution and their capacity for fidelity and love.

Now forty years after the hurricane that destroyed the house where Lisbeth was exiled and died, her daughter, Claire finds herself compelled to bring it back to life. But the past and its evils are awakened as the ruins are disturbed, laying bare the sins of a time when Jim Crow ruled the South, when depravity took place behind lace curtains, and when interracial love could get you killed.

Scan to buy on Amazon

Southern Literary Review Editor, Donna Meredith writes, "This is an award-winning collection of poetry in language so lush and musical it dances across the pages. It offers a profound insight into the meaning of life in a symphony of sound and a kaleidoscope of colors."

"These are gorgeous poems that turn into head-swiveling moments of truth." Phyliss Leichester, author and poet, U.K.

"Brown conducts the moments of everyday life, rich with love and imagination." Josephine Yu, author of *Prayer Book of the Anxious.*

The Leaf Does Not Believe It Will Fall won the 2019 Florida Authors and Publishers Association Silver Medal for Poetry.

Scan to buy on Amazon

Marina Brown, a former hospice nurse, tells the stories of twelve persons who face their last months of life. In these intimate portraits, Brown demystifies the dying process and pulls from it poignancy and beauty. Uplifting and truthful, it is meant for anyone who has ever lost someone and anyone who ever will. Extra pages are provided for the reader to write their own story of someone dear.

Scan to buy on Amazon

A poignant glimpse at this side of the tarmac where travelers leave something of themselves—fragments of living, wishes, hopes, and losses. Here is a collection of Airport characters we've each passed, but never noticed, all captured in stories and vignettes during a week of dawn to dusk encounters. Brown's charcoal sketches help bring them to life.

Made in the USA
Columbia, SC
27 November 2021

49626134R00140